D0050608

OTHER BOOKS BY KATHRYN LASKY

THE SECRET OF GLENDUNNY

❖

Book 1

The Haunting

KATHRYN
LASKY

THE SECRET OF GLENDUNNY

Book 1

The Haunting

HARPER
An Imprint of HarperCollinsPublishers

Library of Congress Control Number: 2021949065
ISBN 978-0-06-303101-2

Typography by Molly Fehr
21 22 23 24 25 SB 10 9 8 7 6 5 4 3 2 1
❖
First Edition

To my grandchildren, Luella, Dashiell, and Errol,
with love from Bama

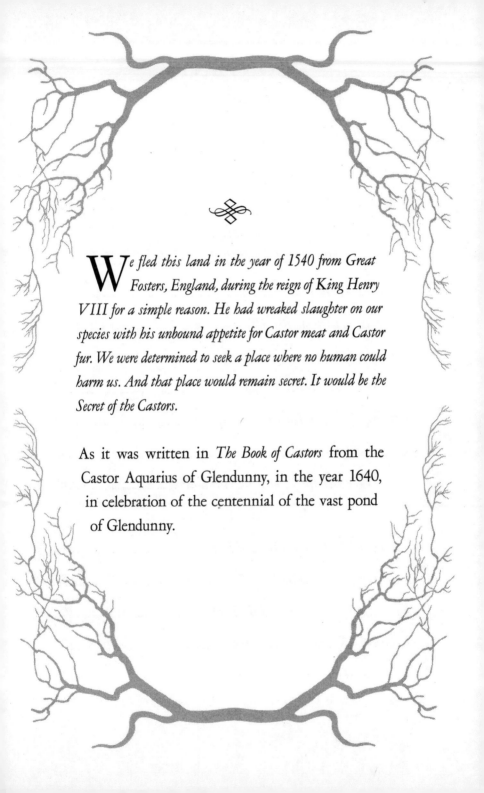

W̲e fled this land in the year of 1540 from Great Fosters, England, during the reign of King Henry VIII for a simple reason. He had wreaked slaughter on our species with his unbound appetite for Castor meat and Castor fur. We were determined to seek a place where no human could harm us. And that place would remain secret. It would be the Secret of the Castors.

As it was written in *The Book of Castors* from the Castor Aquarius of Glendunny, in the year 1640, in celebration of the centennial of the vast pond of Glendunny.

CONTENTS

The Blood Moon

And it came to pass, in the time when the shadow of the earth slides across the moon and the moon appears to bleed red light—yes, in that time, a young beaver kit stirred in his sleep. Deep in his lodge he heard in his dreams a strange new noise. It was not the watery sound of the currents passing slowly through the dam. Nor was it the explosive tail slap of a beaver fracturing the silence of this pond. It was, in fact, a waterless sound. Dry, scraping, and urgent.

Dunwattle's eyes flew open. *This is not a dream. This is real.* But real what? The dry, splintering noise seemed to echo in his ears. Then before him, on the lovely soft pile of shredded bark that was his bed, something white— as white as the birch bark—began to move. There was a rustling, then a low gasping followed by the dry sound.

Bones! Bones like ones he had never before seen. They were not animal—neither weasels nor beavers nor dreaded lynx. These were long bones for standing upright, and this thing was standing right at the end of his bed of shredded birch bark. A two-legs? Impossible!

Time slowed. A strange paralysis overtook poor Dunwattle. He simply could not move. He would not move. He could not scream. He could not even blink. But then he did. Blasted from his soft bed by fear, he hurled himself into the underwater tunnel and out into the stillness of the pond. He swam through the dark, murky waters as long as he could while holding his breath—which was a long time. And then he surfaced, cutting through a tangle of elodea weed. *Away . . . away . . .* That was all he could think as he swam furiously toward a dam . . . any dam!

CHAPTER 1

First Swan

Elsinore, *the mute swan of the Glendunny beaver pond, looked* down from her perch atop the roof of the royal lodge of the Grand Aquarius, the commander in chief of the Castors and this pond. She saw stirrings beneath the carpet of the pond's elodea weed. *By my feathers! Someone's swimming in my soup*, she thought. For indeed it was a delicious variety of algae that was beginning to bloom this time of year, and she didn't relish anyone tearing it apart. It lost its taste when torn. The swans called this particular kind of weed water moss, for it was slightly spongy and very succulent. But the carpet needed to be left undisturbed through the Blood Moon to attain its maximum succulence. All the beavers knew this and were respectful. So the swan wondered why at this hour, nearing the time when beavers would finally cease working, would one be swimming straight through the water moss. Shredding it! *How offensive!*

A nose poked up. Dunwattle! Why would Dunwattle do this? His parents, a lovely couple, would be furious. Elsinore knew that Dunwattle's parents, Grizzmore and Berta, were part of the Chomp at Dam 3 on active maintenance duty. The winter had been rough, with ice floes wreaking damage to all of the eight dams, not to mention the earthquake in late fall that had caused major devastation to countless beaver lodges. If a beaver wasn't repairing—wattling up one with clay, mud, and rock—that beaver was out harvesting new trees for lodge construction. This was the first time Dunwattle and his best friend, Locksley, had been left unattended. They were still young kits and would be for at least another two years. They were only halfway through their kit-hood. So why would Dunwattle be going off like this, and so fast? It appeared as if he were heading toward Dam 8, which was not on the repair schedule for several days.

Elsinore made soft tsk-tsking sounds of disapproval deep in her gullet. She did not gossip. She did not scold. That was not her role at the pond of Glendunny. She observed, she offered some counsel—although there was the new Grand Aquarius: that beaver rarely sought advice. *Mister Know-It-All*, she silently fumed. Had there ever been such a stupid know-it-all? Only stupid creatures pretended to know it all.

And Elsinore knew that there were plenty of stupid creatures in all species.

Since time immemorial, swans and beavers had shared a complicated and fascinating coexistence. This relationship was mutually beneficial. The swans feasted on all the waterweed and delectable treats that the pond offered up, but the pond itself had been created by the beavers. Therefore, the swans returned the favor by providing updates on weather or strangers in the region. At least twice, often three times, a day, Elsinore would fly surveillance and report back to the Grand Aquarius.

He was now called the G. A. for short, instead of the traditional and more modest title, the C. A. That stood for the Castor Aquarius. In the past, the inhabitants of the pond would address this beaver more simply as "Guv'nor," short for governor, or "Guv'ness," if the leader was a female. But no longer. This particular beaver had arrived in his lofty position most literally by accident and refused to be addressed as Guv'nor, but only as "Your Highness." Quite impressed this one was by royalty—human royalty: kings, queens, and all the gaudy nonsense that went along with them. Therefore, the Grand Aquarius sought what he called "treasures" and would commission Elsinore to scour the terrain for such items. In most beavers' minds, these were hardly treasures at all. They were merely useless trinkets. Anything that sparkled or gleamed that might suggest precious gems or gold.

For most beavers, treasures were never trinkets but useful items. Items like mid-growth saplings, which were highly valued and essential for wattling, the woven constructions made from slender branches and filled with mud and often small stones to seal tight a den or a dam. Now those were real treasures, as was the clay known as Great Red. When it was mixed with common mud, it made the best sealant to slather on the interior walls of a lodge.

In fact, what the G. A., His Highness, truly wanted were the castoffs from the humans, whom Castors called two-legs. In particular, the G. A. was drawn to the bits and pieces once owned by especially distinguished or royal two-legs. Gilded frames from pictures were a favorite, as he loved the gold gilt of the wood. Fancy bowls, plates, and dishes from which two-legs ate were other items that delighted him. In short, the Grand Aquarius wanted Elsinore to ransack palatial mansions that had either burned almost to the ground or had been abandoned over the course of hard times. More often the swan would occasionally fly over a particularly rich landfill—those didn't contain priceless items from grand old mansions but simply castoffs. And of course, there were always dumpsters to which bright shiny things occasionally found their way. These would do, as His Highness never knew the difference.

On one flight, Elsinore had found several golden paper crowns. They all had a picture on the front: what looked like a human food with the words "Burger King." More pieces of nonsense for the G. A.'s lodge, which had quickly become a tawdry affair and very unbeaverlike. He adored the paper crowns. Elsinore had found a whole bagful of them, so he could wear a fresh one every few days. She had also found some old broken costume tiaras made for little girl two-legs, after a shop in Shropshire had been flooded. She neglected to tell the G. A. that only little girl royals, princesses, wore tiaras. He wouldn't care, as long as it was shiny and regal in appearance.

The G. A.'s chambers were not lined, as most lodges, with lovely Scotch pine limbs woven together and wattled up to make a cozy chamber for reading or sleeping or studying the water tables. The G. A. did not do much studying. He couldn't be bothered with it. And yet, it was very important for beavers to monitor the water tables of the pond, as they were crucial to the pond's survival. When water was low it meant there was a leak and they quickly had to find it. An S&P, or Search and Plug team, was specially trained for this. If it was not a leak but caused by evaporation from lack of rain, then another stream had to be found and its water flow diverted into the pond.

In addition to all the gewgaws that Elsinore had picked up for this lodge, the G. A. now had a servant too. He had heard about how royal households had staffs: butlers, footmen, and so on. He had no idea what these servants did.

But a half-blind old beaver named Hobbs was brought in to keep things tidy and announce all visitors.

Further duties for Hobbs came to include those of a valet. There was little for Hobbs to do as a valet, since the G. A. had few clothes so far. There were the paper crowns that he changed often so as not to wear them out and the shreds of a velvet cloak that Elsinore had spied on a particularly stinky trash heap miles away, all the way in England, not Scotland, where the Glendunny pond was. Hobbs was a kindly creature and seemed to have infinite patience with the vain old slob. It most likely helped that Hobbs was also half-deaf.

Despite the bizarre behavior of the Grand Aquarius, Elsinore did not complain, nor did she try to correct this behavior. If the pond was happy, she was happy. For now, the G. A. seemed perfectly harmless. The Glendunny pond was finally placid after the violent earthquake in the late fall. Most of the damage from the earthquake had been mended, and there were no longer any aftershock tremors that had followed for several weeks. Things had grown quiet. And most important, the dams were holding. The algae and the pondweed were flourishing. Soon the water lilies would be in bloom and it would be heaven on earth, or as the Castors called heaven, the Great Pond.

Elsinore felt it was useless to point out that it was somewhat silly for the G. A. to have changed his title from

Castor Aquarius, which had served his predecessors for over a thousand years. In changing it to Grand Aquarius, he had swapped his species name for a two-bit adjective. However, she had learned through the years how to pick her battles. Yes, Elsinore might be called mute, simply because she was less vocal than members of other species of swans, but in spite of this she knew a lot of words. She read widely and studied history. Creatures often thought swans were vain because of their grace and beauty, but they hadn't met His Royal Highness the G. A. His vanity was monumental, even though he was just a chunky, furry, leather-tailed creature like the rest of his species. The most conceited animal on earth—so unlike the rest of the Castors. But how had this happened? Before he became His Highness, he had been simply Oscar, Oscar of Was Meadow. *What had happened? How could this change of character be explained?* Elsinore often mused. And where was that young beaver kit Dunwattle heading at this time of the night, so close to dawn?

CHAPTER 2

Clear
Water

Dunwattle was nearing Dam 8. *Through the murky waters, he* could see with his transparent eyelids an old turtle feasting on lily pad roots, and he could hear the croak of wood frogs. He slipped out of the sluggish waters of the pond and scrambled up the steep wall of the dam. Then flinging himself over the top, he slid down the other side. He knew this territory. It was where the elders would first take the kits to learn wattling. He knew that a short distance from here was a stream that ran into a wide creek fringed with willows, where warblers sang in the morning. Should he wait for daylight? It would be safer. Beavers slept most of the day while working through the nights. Dawn was fast approaching, so there would be no lynx lurking about. Lynx were primarily nocturnal. He could not help but think of his grandmother, who had fallen prey to a curse of lynx. Wanda the Wattler, she'd been called.

Wanda's skills were unsurpassable. She could weave together any kind of branches to form the warp of an interior lodge wall. And what a perfect Grand Aquarius she would have made! A calm, steadfast leader. Her end had been a gruesome one that only creatures as vicious as lynx could deliver. A mere scattering of her teeth and very few bones were all that was left. Dunwattle remembered his mum weeping inconsolably as she kept whispering, "Oh, my poor mother. And those teeth. Her lovely incisors! She was born to whittle and wattle."

What was he born to do? Dunwattle was only halfway through his kit-hood, and those bones he saw on the shredded bark of his cozy bed were not incisors. They were bones, the bones of a two-leg—a two-leg that had risen from the dead. A ghost. A *sligh haint* was the old Castor phrase. He couldn't wait around. Lynx or not, if a haint got you . . . He didn't want to think about it! Would it matter that it was just a haint of a two-leg? Was that a lesser violation of the laws of the pond? It was forbidden that a beaver ever be seen by or in the presence of a two-leg—ghost or not. Oh, he couldn't bear to think of it. Once over the dam, he looked around a bit and then bolted for the stream. The water level was up from the snowmelt, and he easily swam down it.

This narrow stream, he realized, led to one of the shunting canals in a spider's web of watercourses. These watercourses were used for transporting the trees that the Chompers felled for building their dams and lodges. Within a few minutes he himself had been shunted into such a canal! At the start he had to swim against the current to get away from Glendunny, but he was a strong swimmer. A better swimmer than a walker, actually. So he swam, dodging floating logs of all sorts. But he was nimble in the water. He loved the sound of the stream's rush, the bubbling tumult of a rapid. The tickle of the water as he feathered his webbed hind feet to avoid the logs or a rock.

Dawn was just breaking as he reached the source of these canals—the River Albyn that would lead him into the Tweed. Soon he heard the loud clamor of a river rapid. He would have to figure out the flanks of the rapid and swim toward the side where the current would not be hard against him. Although he and Locksley had only begun their lessons in water dynamics under Castor Elwyn, he had already learned a lot. Castor Elwyn said that he was one of his best pupils ever. It was the only thing he had ever done better than Locksley, who was a top student in everything, from chomping trees and stripping bark to weaving and wattling.

The water turned white and frothy with the turbulence of the rapids. *Take the rapids at a slant*, the voice of Castor

Elwyn rang in his head. Once across he then swam for all his might toward the calm spot near the edge of the river. Not completely calm, but what Castor Elwyn called *the path of least resistance*. The calm would allow him to escape the current that might pull him back toward those bones of the haint. If he stayed in the calm, he could swim away from all that . . . from the bones that had mysteriously emerged in front of him, materialized in the darkest and deepest part of the night, on that night of the Blood Moon.

He began to feel the change as he swam. He didn't have to work so hard now. His heart did not beat as rapidly as it had from fear and exertion. Dawn was truly breaking now and casting a shimmer of pink over the now-smooth surface of the river. He ducked under, free of the drag of the water. Swimming free of the bones. He had young lungs, but they were good lungs. He could swim for almost a quarter of an hour beneath the surface, holding his breath. "Try for a half quarter: an eighth," his father often said. Dunwattle was not sure what a quarter of a single hour was, let alone an eighth. He had not learned that yet. But the last time he tried, his father had shouted, "You did it! Son, you did it!" And he knew when he was fully grown-up he would be able to swim much longer under the surface.

It took him a bit of time to realize how different the river was from the pond of Glendunny. There was no murk, nor mud. No slime of pond scum or underwater tree stumps. No tangles of pondweed or the slime of elodea vines undulating in dreary brownish water. This water was translucent. He swam through reflections of clouds and blue sky. Then as the sun poured its light, it seemed as if there were a liquid rainbow, turning this underwater landscape into one radiant with colors. He became adept at seeking out the back eddies that swirled against the prevailing current and gave him a boost in the direction he wanted to go. And there was only one way he wanted to go: away. Away from the ghostly haint.

CHAPTER 3

The Strangeness of Oscar of Was Meadow and Other Matters

But now Elsinore was troubled. *Why was little Dunwattle, a gentle soul if there ever was one, taking off like this?* She couldn't follow him, not now. Her duty at this time of the day was to fly in a somewhat tight circumference of the pond to report on any predators. Thugs of the forest. There were all sorts of fangs out there ready to attack Chomps of beavers: wolverines, cougars, brown bears, perhaps even wolves. But no one was quite sure if a wolf population still existed. There were rumors of Rar Wolves in the cedar forest. Rar Wolves were an ancient species of wolves. They were enormous and fearless. It was said they could take down a full-grown bear.

However, oddly enough, the most savage creatures of all

were the smallest: the lynx. A cousin of the bobcat but far more vicious, these creatures with their black tufted ear tips and long deadly fangs were brutal and efficient killers. Some said their oddly translucent green eyes could hypnotize their victims. Bewitched in that gaze of light—the *luma*, they called it—the prey would become instantly paralyzed, totally incapable of movement. Many who had escaped this light said it was as if a curse had been cast upon them. And so indeed, a group of lynx came to be called a "curse" by creatures of the woodlands. And a curse of lynx could shred a beaver in a matter of minutes. Such had been the fate of the G. A.'s predecessor, Wanda the Wattler, Dunwattle's grandmother. She was murdered by a curse of lynx shortly before she was to "Take Lodge," the expression for when a new leader, their Castor Aquarius, was elected.

Elsinore's meandering thoughts were interrupted by a knocking that reverberated up through the drying chamber of the royal lodge. *Oh, flutternuts!* thought the swan. *What does he want now? He should be out working alongside the other beavers.* Setting an example of the industry, hard work that made a beaver a beaver. Diligence was part of their character. Not to mention that there was plenty of work to do since the earthquake. How could a Grand Aquarius build team spirit without working alongside those he ruled? Winter had left a lot of damage. Snowmelt from the mountains would be flooding the pond soon. The Chomps of wattlers for mud plastering would be working through the nights and well into daylight as the new logs and limbs were brought in. So what did that old fool, the G. A., want? And what was that young fool Dunwattle up to? *For every old fool, there's a young fool,* Elsinore thought to herself. She gave a sharp rap with her foot. The signal that she was occupied with "royal business." That was the only excuse she could offer. She was studying a map for her next foraging trip to seek the regal delights that the G. A. relished. And she'd had a sudden thought and wanted to write it down.

Writing for Elsinore was a way of exploring an idea. It helped her sort things out. And she needed to do some sorting out, for she was deeply perplexed about the change in Oscar of Was Meadow. A modest chap with a gentle manner and straightforward way of thinking. Perhaps not the brightest in the Avalinda line of Castor Aquariuses. But kind and dependable. When did this drastic change in his character occur? That was what Elsinore wanted to determine. The time of the change. What phase had the moon been in? What was the water level of the pond? What waterweeds had been blooming? Had a contaminant seeped in directly beneath New Fosters, where the Aquarius lodge stood?

Elsinore stretched her long neck and reached for a diary she kept wedged in between the memoirs of some of her predecessors. It was placed between volumes one and two of *From Damned to Angel: The Story of Byatta, First Swan of Great Fosters.*

Elsinore's diary was actually an old account ledger that she had picked up at a dump several years before. No enticing title, just a rather raggedy red cloth cover with the faded letters "ACCOUNT BOOK." If one opened it, they would not see exactly blank pages but pages with a column format that had a grid of lines for entering numbers. Now after ten years or so, the pages had been written across with actual words and very few numbers, in Elsinore's small but sweeping script. The script would be unintelligible to anyone else, for she wrote in a special language and special alphabet reserved exclusively for swans. The secret language was only for writing and not speaking.

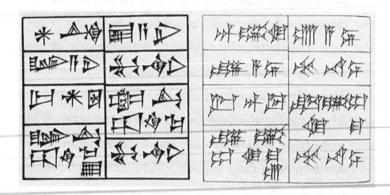

As she wrote these never-spoken words, their twig-ish letters seemed to whisper in her brain.

It has come to me that the G. A. has not always been the pretentious, ridiculous beaver he is now. For the first month of his position as Aquarius, he had none of these airs. He was not the brightest leader we've ever had, but who would have ever suspected this vain creature? I am trying to pinpoint when the change came. Therefore, I am reconstructing the events. Wanda the Wattler was elected to the office during the Maple Moons. She had not officially Taken Lodge yet when she was murdered by a curse of lynx. But there had been one glorious moon first, when the leaves fall from the maple trees and an orangey-red glow the waters of our pond in a tawny glow. Then inexplicably the murder. Oscar of Was Meadow was appointed next, as he had the second-most votes after Wanda. Of course, the beaver who receives the second-most votes is kept a secret. Such is the procedure for succession if a C. A. dies before Taking Lodge. Oscar of Was Meadow was that beaver and served throughout the rest of the Maple Moons. But just as ice began to form, the earthquake happened, and I believe that is when Oscar's peculiar behavior began. He had been such a simple fellow. What could have happened? Did he receive a blow to the head? Large trees were uprooted, rocks had fallen, several dams had collapsed. It had been absolute havoc. A colony of newborn beaver kits had been smothered in a mudslide. And a frail, elderly beaver had been smacked by a giant tree and left flat as his tail.

But Oscar was left without a scratch. So I don't think the earthquake would explain it. Oscar is always slow in his ways. But then the quake happened, and this dull, tedious beaver became foolish ... dare I say fatuous with his ideas. Complete delusions of grandeur.

Gentle knocks reverberated up from the ceiling of the G. A. lodge to the roof where Elsinore's nest was. "Hobbs here, Elsinore. His Highness is eager for your opinion on the royal lounging slippers you brought him. Might they be worn as a royal nightcap when he is not wearing the crown?"

"Oh yes, of course . . . er . . . Tell him that Charles the Second often wore his slippers on his head. Nothing better for a good night's sleep—even during the day, as you beavers do."

Elsinore clamped her eyes shut. *The things I have to deal with!*

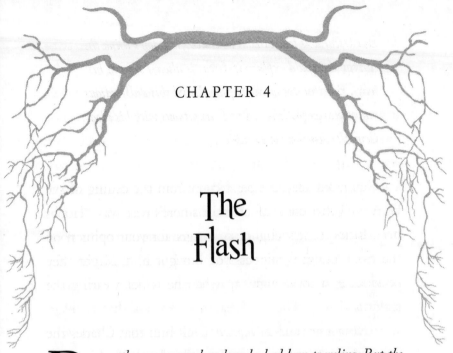

CHAPTER 4

The Flash

Dunwattle *was unsure how long he had been traveling. But the* sun was now setting, and he had left quite a bit before dawn. Even though the current had been against him part of the way, he must have covered a lot of distance. Time perhaps for a rest. He was hungry and pondweed did not thrive in rivers. Nor were there any sticks floating about. He would have to go onto the land and find a few slim branches and tender trees to gnaw. Maybe some woody shrubs as an appetizer.

Dunwattle wasn't really inclined to emerge from the water. After all, it had been drilled into all the Castors of Glendunny that their pond and their dams were secrets never to be revealed. If two-legs ever found them, they were doomed. They were safe where they were, where the two-legs never came.

Why they never came to Glendunny, no one really knew. It was never explained to them in the school lodge. "They just don't!" Castor Feltch said. Feltchie, as the kits called her, was a snappish old beaver and the teacher of scumology, a complicated subject that focused on all the varieties of pondweed that could flourish in a healthy pond. "Muck is my business," she would often say. "And keeping this pond in tip-top health is my passion." But it seemed keeping the pond secret was everyone's passion, and yet they were never really told why. The only reason given was that two-legs were dangerous and never came to Glendunny. But why wouldn't the two-legs come? If a kit asked such a question, and only kits did, they were scolded severely. Sometimes they could even be punished—not allowed to participate in certain festivals, such as the spring moons creek run festivals. Or not allowed eat the scrumptious fiddlehead ferns and the baby ones that were just beginning to unfurl. In fact, that first month of the spring moons was called the Month of the Callow Ferns. And it was followed by the Month of the Tender Bark. Such feasting they would have! And of course, the water dancing was the best part. But naughty beaver kits would be "logged." And to be logged was the worst: a kit would have to sit on a log and watch while his mates danced in celebration of the high waters.

A dancer would find a rhythm in the depths of the pond or the current of a river—then they would slap their tail to the beat and invite another beaver to join the dance. Then more and more beavers would swim out to where the two beavers had started the swirling water dance and join in. All except for the kits who had broken some rule. Many of these rules had to do with the secret history of the pond. And the gravest of all these rules was that of *vysculf*: no beaver was ever to be seen by a two-leg. The penalty for such a violation was expulsion from the pond, or worse. Some even whispered that the punishment was actually execution, by a curse of lynx. But it seemed to be just a rumor. For the death of Wanda the Wattler had certainly not been a punishment.

The Castorium made the rules, the laws that had been created almost four centuries ago. But the elders of the Castorium would never answer questions about why a beaver could never be seen by a two-leg. It was all part of the history of the pond. The reason had come to be called the Secret of Glendunny. It drove Dunwattle's best friend, Locksley, crazy. "How can they expect us to obey these rules if we don't know why they are there?" he would fume. Locksley was always pushing. Always asking why. *Ahh, Locksley,* Dunwattle thought. He missed him already. More than once a Castor had told Locksley he was too curious for his own good. It would make Dunwattle shiver when they said that, but it didn't seem to deter his friend.

And now he himself was possibly guilty of breaking that biggest rule of all. He could tell he was far from the pond. The water was somehow very different. Strange and slightly alien. There was not a trace of those streams and rivers that fed the pond of Glendunny.

And this seemed to put an edge to his hunger. *I'm starving!* Dunwattle thought. He poked his head out of the water to survey the food possibilities. Everything was so luminous. Too luminous, almost. Too few shadows. No murk in the water if he needed to dive deep should a lynx appear. Liquid rainbows and reflections of fluffy clouds were pretty, but you sure couldn't eat them and one couldn't hide in them either.

If he wanted to eat, he'd have to scramble up a bank. The water was simply too clean, too clear here. There wasn't even a speck of alga. He felt a twinge of homesickness. Where were the other pond creatures that he knew so well? The water striders that skimmed across the surface and sometimes landed on his nose. The splendid polka-dot frog that posed on water lilies. The dignified mallard ducks with their train of little ducklings following so obediently behind their mother. They all lived together in perfect pond harmony. Dunwattle would never consider a duck or even a water flea to be food. Beavers were strictly vegetarian. Wood and pond greens. That was their diet.

He surveyed the bank. There were some tempting gray alders up there. It wouldn't take much time to chomp a couple down. Their trunks were slender. He could make quick work of the nearest one. Dunwattle thought he might prefer something a tad sweeter, but hey, beggars can't be choosers. *And I,* he thought, *am definitely a beggar.* He poked his nose through the surface one more time to survey the food possibilities. His paw had just hit the slippery bank when there was a blinding flash. The world went white. An electrical white like during a summer storm. Dunwattle froze, blinded by this horrendous brightness. He blinked. He felt a twinge in his deep gut, in his *skeat,* the pouch that would break down the wood he hoped to be chewing. But this harsh light was not like wood. It would not break down for easy digestion. In fact, he experienced just the opposite. He was suddenly nauseous. On the brink of throwing up. Beavers often experienced their strongest emotions in their digestive tract. The hot, blistering whiteness of the flash began to clear and what was left was even worse. A bespectacled two-leg peering directly at him, murmuring.

"My! My! My! I can hardly believe my eyes. A beaver! A beaver in England!"

I can hardly believe my eyes, Dunwattle thought. *I've done it. I've been seen. Vysculf. I am vysculf. I shall be banished or . . . or . . . even worse, executed!*

Meanwhile the two-leg was whispering rather loudly

to herself. "No one will believe me! Not without a photo."

I hope they don't, Dunwattle thought desperately. And then the woman lifted a peculiar device again to her eye and there was another blinding flash, but by this time Dunwattle had already ducked into the water and was gone. The last thing he heard her say was, "Oh my stars, I can't wait to tell the world about this!"

Dunwattle seemed to freeze in the water with his mouth wide open. He felt himself begin to sink, sink like a stone. *I might as well die now. I'd rather drown then be torn apart by lynx. I am doomed, utterly doomed.*

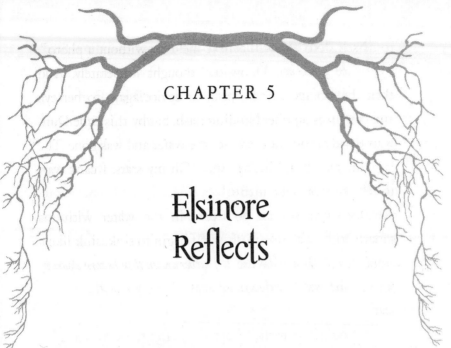

CHAPTER 5

Elsinore
Reflects

Elsinore *was worried. Dunwattle had left the pond hours before,* almost an entire day. Now it was deep twilight, and Locksley had been by twice to ask if she had seen him. She lied of course and made some frail excuse that perhaps he had gone to work on Dam 3 with his parents. "You know, the first time staying all by yourself in the lodge can be a bit frightening."

"Not for me," Locksley replied.

"But you had your grandma Thwistle there."

"Grandma Thwistle is so old! What could she ever do to protect me? She's lost both her incisors. She can hardly chew anything. And she's almost blind. Not to mention deaf."

"Now don't speak that way about your grandma. She's a dear old soul and knows so many wonderful stories. I would expect more from you, young Locksley. Dunwattle lives down by Puddle-No-More, doesn't he? It's rather isolated there. So maybe he went to his cousins' lodge."

"Yes, ma'am." Locksley dipped his head and was immediately contrite. Kits oftentimes listened to Elsinore more than they did to their own parents or teachers. Elsinore seemed to be able to say things to kits that their parents could not without having a squabble. It was most likely because she was a different species. "Now you swim along, dear."

"All right," he replied. "But I'm going to be so bored."

"No B word, please. You know how I loathe the B word. Go out and gnaw a birch."

"I'm not hungry."

"Well, gnaw it just for the pleasure of gnawing. Gnaw it for art. Did you see that stunning sculpture Dunwattle made?"

"The one of the mother duck with her little ducklings?"

"No. Although that was nice, but I prefer his more abstract ones. The piece he called *Storm Raging*. Magnificent! You could feel the power of the wind."

"I . . . I don't understand that kind of art—what do you call it? Abstract?"

"Yes, abstract."

"What does that mean?"

Elsinore tipped her lovely head to one side. She shut one eye so that it seemed to disappear entirely into the black feathers that grew in a distinct pattern around her eyes.

"Hmmm...," Elsinore mused. "It means something that is emotional and not just concrete. It touches your deepest feelings." She sighed. "And to make such art I believe one has to have deep feelings."

"But what then is 'concrete'?" *Oh dear*, Elsinore thought. These beavers knew so little of the rest of the world. She herself flew far and wide and had seen so much: concrete buildings along with brick ones, sidewalks and paving stones. "It means . . . it means it's more about feelings than just mud and wattling, logs and limbs, rocks and dams. There are no real rules with abstract art."

"I'd like that!" Locksley said.

"Yes, I guess you would. I am familiar with your contempt for rules."

"But I'm not artistic like Dunwattle."

"You could be if you tried. Now stop whining."

Elsinore began to fluff up her feathers, and Locksley retreated. It didn't pay to provoke a swan. They were massively powerful. Not that Elsinore would ever hurt a creature. Unless it was a two-leg trying to up her. Both Locksley and Dunwattle loved Elsinore's upping stories. Before she had come to Glendunny, she had been "upped."

She had explained that in England the ruling monarch officially owned all the swans in the kingdom. Every year, the king's or queen's swan uppers would go out in their skiffs on the river to count the swans for something called a "census." Elsinore had been upped, or counted, as a young cygnet. The uppers had placed a ring around her leg. It was still on her leg when she first arrived at Glendunny, but Castor Elwyn, or E. B. as she called him, had delicately gnawed it off her leg without even leaving a scratch. She had saved it and would reattach it when she went on particularly long and detailed flyovers near London. The uppers would leave her be when they saw the ring, as they would know she had already been counted for the census. Elsinore derived a special delight in fooling two-legs. She didn't want those grubby fellows netting her again.

Almost the moment Locksley left, Elsinore heard a grunt from below. It issued from the top of the Grand Aquarius's lodge, directly beneath Elsinore's nest.

"Oh good grief, not again!" the swan muttered.

"You're needed, Elsinore," another voice called out. It was Hobbs, the G. A.'s servant.

Elsinore squirmed through an entry tunnel to the presence chamber, where the Grand Aquarius received visitors. As required by him, she scraped her way toward the throne that the fat old beaver sprawled upon. His Burger King crown had slipped down, almost covering one eye. Just as the crown was not truly a crown, the throne was not a throne but a seat assembled from remains of a discarded gilt picture frame and a gilt dinner chair. These had been found floating in the river and retrieved by a Chomp of scrappers. The chair had no seat but still had its four legs and a back. Yet it was unsteady. So both the frame and the seatless chair had been set on a nice squarish rock that helped balance them. There were some interesting marks gouged on the stone, an inscription of some sort. No one had really bothered to try and decipher it.

Beavers often found useful items delivered by the flotsam of a river—discarded automobile tires, fragments of metal—but in this case, the wood of the chair and the picture frame had been gilded, so the beavers considered them too flashy for their lodges or dams. Yet nothing was too flashy for the G. A.'s personal use. Most of the beavers and other pond inhabitants found these royal delusions of the G. A. peculiar at best, for beavers are modest animals that prefer to blend in seamlessly with their surroundings. Such was not the case with the G. A.

Elsinore, pressing her belly to the floor, inched forward. This royal protocol had never before been demanded in the history of beavers, but ever since Elsinore had found a damaged copy of a book, *Fit for a Queen: A Guide to Royal Etiquette*, the Grand Aquarius had become obsessed with the rules, customs, and traditions of the courts of ruling monarchs of the British Empire.

"How may I serve you, Your Majesty?" Elsinore asked.

"Didn't you once tell me that the monarch of England owned all the swans in the British Isles?"

"Yes I did, Your Majesty."

"And did you not tell me that he or she . . ."

"Her name is Elizabeth. Queen Elizabeth."

"Yes, that she had a special title due to this? An additional name or well . . . whatever?"

"Yes," Elsinore said, trying to disguise the weariness in her voice.

"And what is that title?"

"The Seigneur of the Swans."

"Indeed! What a ring it has to it."

Yes, a ring is the problem, Elsinore thought. *Ring around my foot!* This was becoming more uncomfortable by the second.

"Well, since I own you, I think it only appropriate that you address me as 'Seigneur de Cygne.' French, you know, for swan. French is . . ." The beaver shrugged his massive shoulders. "Well, you know, more . . . more . . . like. Oh, you know that king you told me about, Louis . . . ?"

"King Louis the Fourteenth."

"Exactly! He's one of my favorite monarchs."

"Of course," Elsinore muttered.

"Oh, I'm glad you agree."

"But I don't agree."

"You don't agree! How can you not agree with the Grand Aquarius?"

"It's quite simple. You don't own me. I serve here of my own free will."

"Oh no!" The beaver sighed. A tear trickled down through his furry face.

"Don't despair. I have another idea for a title." Elsinore was a quick thinker.

"For me?" His eyes lit up with delight. "And what's that?"

"You'll love it. Many more letters but the same amount of syllables as Majesty."

"Syllables? What's a syllable?"

"Never mind. Here's the title." The beaver's eyes shone bright in anticipation. "His Eagerness," Elsinore whispered as if she were disclosing a precious secret.

"His Eagerness." The Grand Aquarius whispered the name. "Yes, yes. It appeals to me."

It appalls, thought Elsinore.

"I like it. A lovely little hiss sound at the end."

"That's due to the double S in the word."

"All right, all right. I like it very much. I shall issue a decree."

"You do that! It's now time for my twilight surveillance flight. Bonsoir, Your Eagerness." A light twinkled in the

G. A.'s eyes. He loved it when Elsinore spoke French. So elegant. Elsinore then swept her port wing. For this was how swans curtseyed.

The swan emerged from the presence chamber and immediately took wing, flying south by southeast. She could not help but think about her recent diary entry. Was the earthquake somehow a key to this change in character of the G. A.? The beaver formerly known as Oscar of Was Meadow? Although he was a descendant of Avalinda, the hallowed beaver of Great Fosters, he was not a direct descendant. Still, he was close enough to be eligible for the office of the Aquarius, even if his upbringing had been humble. He had been a good Chomp member, specialized in stripping bark, allowing branches to swell quickly for wattling. In fact he even directed the swell pools, where logs floated for a few days so they could absorb as much water as possible. Well-swelled logs, or "plumps" as they were called, made for a tight fit when slapping on the mud for wattling.

Now he did nothing. Except for his bizarre preoccupation with royalty and royal trappings, he lazed about all day and all night. He had even taken to sleeping at night, which was rare for many animals and unheard of for beavers. Night was their best work time. He might be the Grand Aquarius, His Majesty, His Highness, His Eagerness, but he certainly was a lousy beaver. A failed beaver, if there ever was one. And now, just a scant few months since the earthquake, he was definitely His Lousiness! Had his brain been jiggled in some irreparable way? A brainquake?

Elsinore put these thoughts aside and within a few minutes she spied Dunwattle—he was swimming at breakneck speed up the fast stream of a shunting canal. Canal number 58. Where had he been? And why? Even from this altitude, Elsinore detected that there was something desperate, fraught—almost wretched—as the beaver swam toward the pond. What had the poor kit seen? *Or*—and the thought was like a cold knife in Elsinore's gizzard—*had he perchance been seen?*

CHAPTER 6

Seen!

The flash had been like a punch in Dunwattle's skeat or perhaps his brain, or maybe both. As Dunwattle swam away from the shore, it was as if that blinding light still sizzled inside him. He could not help but think of poor Grammy Wanda. Was this what it was like for her when she was caught by the lynx, trapped in the luma of the paralyzing green light? The few creatures who had escaped the luma said it was as if an evil spell had been cast upon them. It locked their joints, slowed their blood and the pumping of their hearts, until they could not breathe or even shriek as the horrible fangs of the lynx ripped their flesh. *But I am swimming!* Dunwattle thought. *Two paws, four paws are pulling me through this water.* His tail was ruddering as a tail should.

The blistering white light was dissolving.

The water had changed. It was not so clear now. How thrilled Dunwattle was to taste the tang of the murk and the slime of weed. How peaceful he felt in the dusky gloom of the sludge waters as he neared Glendunny. The dim pulse of the canal as opposed to the wild beating heart of a tumultuous river. How could he have ever reveled in those bright waters? Give him shadows and the silty smell of mud laced with wattling clay. Give him the caress of the tangles of elodea vines swaying in the currents. Oh! He was almost home! And yet of course he was frightened. He had been seen. Twice now: once by a ghost and now by a real, live human being. No one could ever find out. He could not even tell Locksley. Absolutely no one should ever know what he had seen and or rather who had seen him. Would they smell it? Would he have the scent of a two-leg on him? But the two-leg had never touched him. Nevertheless, his fur had been drenched in those clear, sparkling waters. Would he carry that smell with him? He dived and burrowed in the delicious mud of the canal.

Oh my, Dunwattle thought as he rolled and spun and grubbed about in the glorious, fantastic slime of the canal bottom. *It feels so good to be home! There is nothing, absolutely nothing finer than this mudlucious squishiness!*

And then suddenly he smelled the slime of the pond

trickling through Dam 8. He scrambled over the dam and slipped into the pond. He was home. Home at last!

The fireflies had come out. One flashed directly beneath Dunwattle. Oh good, it was FF2 language. The one firefly language that Dunwattle understood. There were at least three species of fireflies in the pond, and each kind had its own language. Flashes were their words. Some flashed dot . . . dot . . . dash all in a line while others performed an intricate zigzag dance. This firefly was luckily flashing in dot dash dash dot: . —. It meant, "Hello, Dunwattle. Where you been?" But he didn't bother to answer and rushed on.

He scrambled over Dam 8 and headed straight for the other end of the pond, a region called Was Heath, where Locksley's family lodge had been built. With any luck Locksley's parents were still away working on Dam 3 with Dunwattle's parents. Dunwattle swam through the water entrance and staggered up the incline to the level of the sleeping chambers. He was not quiet. Not at all. And he heedlessly dripped mud over the thick pelt of new moss Locksley's mother had laid down.

Locksley poked his head out of the sleeping chamber. "What in the name of Great Castor . . . and . . ." He looked at the mud-stained carpet of moss. "Mum's going to . . ."

But as he crouched there looking at his best friend, Dunwattle knew he was going to have to tell Locksley the truth of what had happened.

"Dunwattle . . . you . . . you look . . . scared. Really scared."

It was as if the breath had locked in Dunwattle's throat, but then that single word burst out. *"Vysculf!"*

Confusion swam in Locksley's eyes. "Wh . . . wh . . . ?" It was as if his mouth could not form the word, could not find the shape of the sound.

"Locksley, I've been seen!"

"Vys . . . vys." Locksley struggled to say it. He could not utter the whole word, and there was only one real word for what had happened to Dunwattle. It was vysculf, that old Castor word that meant, "seen by a two-leg." Or what the rest of the world called a "human being."

"Yes, vysculf. . . . I've been seen by a two-leg."

Locksley's eyes reflected a terrorizing darkness, as bad or worse than the scalding whiteness that Dunwattle had experienced when the two-leg had made that flash with the object she carried. Locksley's orange chisel-shaped front teeth began to click—it sounded almost like the death clack that some say dying beavers make. His thick furry lips appeared as if they were trying to find the shape of the word. And then finally Locksley blurted it out. "Vvvv . . . vvv . . . vysculf."

Dunwattle nodded, and although he was shivering with fear, he felt a hot shame race through him. He looked down.

There seemed to be a long silence. "I'll have to leave," he murmured. He felt the stroke of the grooming claw with the special nail comb on Locksley's hind foot. It raked lightly through his shoulder fur. So lovely, that feeling. It calmed him a bit.

"No . . . no . . . ," Locksley said softly, his voice still trembling. "But tell me, Dunwattle, how did this happen? Where did it happen?"

"I . . . I . . . I just . . . Well, I was kind of bored . . . and I just thought I'd go out for a swim, you know." He looked up into Locksley's black eyes. Locksley tried to hold his gaze. Dunwattle could tell exactly what his best friend was thinking. *This is not the whole story. What is Dunwattle leaving out?* But even though Dunwattle sensed it, he was too frightened to say anything. But then Locksley spoke, very softly.

"Dunwattle, when you're ready, tell me the whole story." He spoke calmly and took a step back, settling on his broad flat tail as if he had all day to listen.

"Ready? Ready for what?" Dunwattle said innocently.

"As I said, ready to tell me the whole story."

Dunwattle sighed deeply and settled on his own rather narrow, hairless tail. He wished his tail were larger, fatter. But the shape of beaver tails varies from family to family, and Dunwattle had inherited the classic Mumpsluff tail from his father's side of the family. He sighed and wondered how he could explain to his best friend what had happened. He might as well just spit it out. Spit it out as if he had accidently swallowed a fish or a frog.

"Well, what did you mean, exactly?" Locksley exclaimed.

"Sorry, I'm a bit nervous. . . ."

"What's wrong, Dunwattle?"

"Uh, um, bones . . . the bones!" He said what he had known all the time but had not wanted to admit. The thing, the force that had driven him from his comfy bed in his family's lodge. The bones. "A ghost. They were the bones of a ghost, the ghost of a two-leg. A haint!" The bones of a dead two-leg were what had propelled him to leave, to end up falling into that terrible flash of light, to be seen by the live two-leg. This was going to be hard to explain.

He shut his eyes and saw those bones so clearly once again. Saw it all. The bones belonged to a child, a child that was perhaps close to his own age. A girl child. He was sure. Dunwattle had begun to speak softly. He felt Locksley edge in closer and resettle once more on his own admirably broad, fat tail. Then he draped his short foreleg around Dunwattle's shoulders. It helped. The story came out more smoothly as Dunwattle disclosed the horrific events to his best friend, perhaps his only true friend in Glendunny, and how later those agonizing seconds—for it was only a matter of seconds—culminated in the white flash when the two-legs spotted him.

"Please explain, Dunwattle. What exactly did you see? An actual, living two-legs or the ghost of one?"

"Both," Dunwattle replied succinctly. "It was the ghost that drove me out of my den and right into a true, living two-legs on the banks of a river far from here." It was as if he had been propelled by the dead to the living.

"You're sure it was a two-legs?"

"What else could it be with two legs? And it was a she—a female—and dressed in clothes, just as Castor Helfenbunn taught us in Two-legs Vigilance class. And so was the ghost, but her clothes were all tattered and . . . and bloody!" Dunwattle took a deep breath. "Both were human beings." He concluded. The two beavers remained silent for a good while. And then Locksley looked up and spoke.

"We need to go to Elsinore."

"Elsinore?"

"Yes, Elsinore. She will know what to do," Locksley replied quietly.

"At this hour of the night?" Dunwattle asked.

"We'll wait until morning. She gets grouchy when awakened."

"But we have wattling class with Castor Tonk, and we can't be late. She hates me, I think. All because I'm the grandson of Wanda, the greatest wattler ever!"

"Don't worry. We'll get to Elsinore before the end of the day." But all Locksley could think was that Elsinore, the normally imperturbable swan, might definitely be perturbed when they told her this news.

Meanwhile far away from the site of the catastrophic event that Dunwattle had endured, Adelaide McPhee could not sleep. She had not slept since that historic occurrence on the banks of the Tweed. Although she had just turned forty, she realized that this could make her career. She tried to shut her eyes, but all she saw was that adorable face of Dunwattle peering up at her. Every five minutes it seemed, she had to get up from her bed and look at the picture. Just one more day and spring break would be over. For ten years she had been researching Rodentia Diversity, or biological differences in rodents, of England and Europe. And she researched mostly rats, for they were the most available of all species of Rodentia. There were 2,052 rat species alone. She had actually done extensive research on a strain of rats that had brought the bubonic plague to England during the time of Shakespeare. But she in fact had always wanted to explore that elusive semiaquatic species of rodents known as castors. Beavers! But there were none in England. Would people believe that she had actually seen one? They had to believe. She had the picture—three pictures.

Although she was the Michael Hammersley Professor of Rodentia Diversity, she was really tired of rats. But beavers were not simply elusive; they were gone from England.

How she longed to study them and their family life and the rearing of their kits. She was sick of the family life and social organization of rats. Not only did they cause plagues of historic proportions, but they ate their young, for heaven's sake. Not always, of course, but often enough. She had written her thesis on that dreadful topic. Cannibalism among rats. The specific object of her thesis was *Rattus norvegicus*, which did not actually evolve in Norway as its name might suggest but in Northern Asia.

However, *Castor canadensis*—beavers! My goodness! No baby eating for them. Beavers were engineers, builders, creators of wetlands, preservers of wetlands, and wonderful parents. Years ago when she was at the beginning of her career, she would have had to go to North America to research them. But the university had said it was too expensive to support this venture. She had thought of asking her great-aunt Glencora, who was very rich, but her husband had just died quite suddenly, and she didn't want to ask her for money at a time of such monumental grieving.

Adelaide looked at her bedside clock. *Just four more hours,* she thought, *then I'll meet with my lab.* She had already reserved a meeting room. But she had not yet revealed the reason.

Four hours later she walked into McDuff Laboratories at New Cavendish University in Scotland. She set up her laptop on the lectern, then plugged in the wire for the video projection screen. Two dozen or so people from her lab were streaming into the auditorium.

"Must be something special, Adelaide?" An ancient and distinguished professor of rat communities in the outer boroughs of London came up to her.

"Very special, professor," Adelaide replied. "I'd say it made my holiday break."

A very well-dressed woman, Phylis Whitby, professor of social dynamics in families of porcupines and muskrats, was standing by him. "Well, well, let's get started."

Adelaide waited a minute or so more until the various professors and their graduate students settled down. She then cleared her throat and stood behind the lectern and rubbed her hands lightly as if relishing what she was about to say.

"I hope you all had a lovely holiday break. And I am so excited to share this truly astonishing news with you today." She paused briefly and looked at the ceiling as if anticipating that some words equal to this occasion would drop right into her mouth. "I feel this is . . . dare I say . . . an historic moment, a cataclysmic one in the history—" She broke off her speech abruptly. Then laughed gaily. "Don't want to give it all away yet. I want you to see first something I came across during break while walking a path along the lower River Tweed earlier this month." She now nodded to Jean, her lab assistant, to dim the lights, then pressed a key on her laptop computer. There was a collective gasp as Dunwattle's face loomed large on the screen. His black eyes shined, his huge teeth glistened almost gold.

"Along the lower Tweed?" someone called out.

"Indeed, Mr. Murphy." She paused. "And here's another of the same beaver." She had definitely captured the startled look in Dunwattle's eyes. And then the third shot caught his tail slapping the water and a rain of sparkling droplets exploding from the calm surface of the river.

"B-b-b-b . . . b-b-but . . ." Phylis Whitby rose from her seat and was stammering. "There hasn't been a beaver sighting in England since . . ."

"The reign of Henry the Eighth," Adelaide replied quickly. "They began to disappear between King Henry's third and fourth wife. His third wife was Jane Seymour and his fourth wife was Anne of Cleves. Gossip had it that Anne of Cleves was not known for her beauty and that her face actually reminded Henry of a beaver. He went on a rampage trying to kill the creatures—as opposed to killing his wife, as he had been known to do—hence the remaining few beavers disappeared almost overnight to escape his wrath and his hunger for their meat and furs." Adelaide McPhee had been an ardent student of English history and the Tudor dynasty, the family dynasty of King Henry, before she had turned to biology.

"So now they're back?" a student asked.

"Well, at least one is back. I did not have to go to Canada to find this fellow."

"Fellow, you feel? It's male?"

"I think so, judging by the size. Though I didn't see this one out of the water. But it seemed small as compared to pictures I have seen of females. As you may or may not know, female beavers are larger than males. I plan to apply for research grants. The research study most likely will be expensive, as I feel we will need to purchase at least three drones."

"Ah . . . ," someone said. "Eyes in the sky, I suppose."

"Exactly what we need—eyes in the sky flying surveillance over this territory."

She now showed a map on the screen. There was an X on the map marking the spot where she had encountered Dunwattle. "The river flows east at a slant. I was staying in Peebles with my great-aunt Glencora. But this young fellow—pardon me, castor—could have been coming from the south or possibly the north, against the current, I think. I have no idea. To the north the woods thicken; the hills build into mountains. I think it might be hard for a drone, that eye in the sky, to see anything. If anyone would like to join me in this endeavor, if you are tired of rats or porcupines or squirrels, I think it would make for a grand adventure. The social dynamics of a beaver's life promise to be fascinating."

By the end of her presentation almost half the audience signed up to join the endeavor, as she called it. And Adelaide herself would dream of castors every night for the rest of the summer. *Castor Britannia*, as she thought of them. Oh, to name a species, the dream of any biologist. *Castor Britannia McPheeus*, in the Linnaean system of classification of living things. Definitely castor fever had set in on the campus of New Cavendish University. Dozens wanted to sign up. And Professor McPhee's applications for grants were met with success. She might be able to buy those drones by the end of the summer.

CHAPTER 7

A Ghostly Visitor

*A*t the opposite end of the pond from *Was Heath, there was a* swampy quarter known as Lower Scum. This was where the New World beavers lived, the Cass Canucks who had immigrated from Canada two hundred years or so before. And there sat an orphan beaver known as Yrynn, reclining on her bedding of moss, leaves, and tattered bark. She was waiting. Waiting patiently for the bones that she knew would appear. First the bones would emerge in a jumble, and then a mist would rise from the muddled pile. Gradually these bones—the ribs, the anklebones, and those of the hands and feet—would begin to sort themselves out of their higgledy-piggledy heaps and eventually reassemble themselves into a shape. The shape of a two-legs. And if both—both sets of bones, that is—would come, there would be two-legs squared! Yrynn was a natural-born mathematician. At least that's what Castor Feltch said. Feltch was the only beaver teacher who was nice to her in the whole darn pond.

In general, nobody was very nice to the Canucks. They were considered "upstarts"—well, that was the kindest word. Upstarts, immigrants, foreigners, or "furrinors"—as their fur was considered beautiful. Their pelts were so desirable that for this reason Yrynn's ancestors had fled Canada, where they had all been mercilessly hunted down for their pelts. The pelts were then turned into beaver hats that were considered quite elegant at one time. Such hats had become the rage two hundred years or so before. Entire beaver populations in the New World were slaughtered to near extinction. The only escape from becoming a hat was to leave and leave fast. Thus, a few "Cass Canucks" came over by sneaking aboard an eastbound sailing vessel. Yrynn's ancestors had been among those brave Castors. Indeed one of Yrynn's relatives, her great-great-great-grandmother, had written a book, a memoir entitled *Outrage!* The subtitle was *My Husband Is Now a Hat.*

Despite this sad history, the Canuck Castors had never truly been accepted. Grown-up Canuck beavers were shunned. They could not be admitted to the Castorium, the highest governing council of the Glendunny pond.

The only beaver who was at all nice to Yrynn was Castor Feltch, who spent a lot of time in Lower Scum analyzing the various weeds that flourished there. She had come to know the young Canuck and saw how bright she was. And of course there was Kukla, the librarian. Kukla liked Yrynn because she read. Kukla loved kits who read. And she was fascinated by the stories that Yrynn has shared with her, the stories her parents had told her, called the Spirit Legends. "You must write them down, Yrynn dear. You really must," Kukla had told her. But the problem was that Yrynn's parents had both disappeared on a willowing expedition during her first year. Willows were the favorite food of beavers, and they hoarded the slender succulent branches for the time of the Hunger Moons. It was feared that a wolf pack had brought them down. Since then, Yrynn had basically raised herself. She tried desperately to hold in her head—or in her mind's eye, as her mum said—all those spirit stories her parents had told her. But sometimes it seemed as if they were fading. And there was another problem too. The Spirit Legends came from Canada. She knew if some beavers knew this, they would be disdainful. So she kept them to herself, but each day she would whisper the stories to herself to keep them safe in her memory.

Canucks were allowed to gather food and help with sherding. Sherding was not to be confused with shredding, which was how they tore bark to eat or mix with mud for wattling. But sherding was a job that required great skill—it involved guiding or herding big logs down turbulent rivers. No Castor could shove and guide a big log down a river like a Canuck. They had lived in a world on the far side of the ocean that had wild rivers and forests with trees so enormous that it was impossible to imagine. Giant logs were vital for the creation of a pond, not just to allow for flooding but for the construction of dams and lodges. With their fantastic teeth, beavers could gnaw them down to whatever size needed. And they could float a log down a river like no other creature. There were many myths. Some say the Cass Canucks had originally learned this skill from two-legs who cut trees and "danced them down turbulent rivers." And that was part of the ancestral memory that had come with them from Canada. Yrynn was a log dancer herself. But did they appreciate her? No, she was greeted only with suspicion.

"How did she learn that?" some Glendunny beavers would often wonder aloud as they watched her.

"Verrry strange . . . indeed."

"She's an orphan—who would have taught her?"

"Perhaps she's a witch, a *maranth*." Beavers could be a superstitious lot, and some Castors were deeply suspicious. They had a curse for every occasion. If a tree fell the wrong way, making it hard to transport, it was said a hex had been cast upon it. When Yrynn overheard Tonk, a wattle, say this, she felt a shiver run through her. But she was away from all that now. And maybe her new friend would come on the light of the dawn. That was her usual time. If they knew about her new friend, Tonk and the others would certainly think Yrynn was a maranth.

Nevertheless, she watched with delight as the mist begin to rise at the end of her bed. *My friend the haint is coming. She's coming!* Yrynn thought. Which of the Spirit Legends should she whisper into the creeping glow that was beginning to swirl at the end of her bark bed? Perhaps the one of Little Blue and Little Kit, the wandering stars that blazed in the Canadian sky. But she could never tell the stories quite the way her mother had. She always felt that she was leaving something out. Soon, she heard a dry, rustling sound. It was working!

"Lorna?" she whispered.

"Yes, Yrynn."

Oh! To hear her name spoken with such warmth thrilled her. Before the earthquake, she always felt she was just whispering these stories into the void, but since the quake it had all changed; her life had changed in such a wonderful way. For many it had been a disaster, but for Yrynn it was the moment she first met Lorna, this ghost girl, in her tattered dress. Lorna had come to hear her stories. Yrynn was unsure how long she had been listening before she actually showed herself. Lorna didn't care if sometimes Yrynn forgot parts of a story. Yrynn herself was getting better at filling in the missing bits and pieces. Lorna seemed always to shimmer a bit brighter when Yrynn would begin another Little Blue and Little Kit story. "Once upon a time," she would whisper, "in the great North Woods of Canada, there was a beaver kit and a little wolf pup who had wandered afar from their lodge in the sky. . . ."

Sometimes when she forgot an important part of the story she would get teary and have to break off.

"Don't worry, " Lorna would say. "It's still a good story."

"But my mum had told me that once the little wolf pup had a second name, a real name, and not just Little Blue."

"It doesn't matter," Lorna replied. "You are such a good storyteller, I feel as if I know the creature."

Nevertheless, the lost name prickled Yrynn's dreams while she slept. She wished she could remember it. But it was storytelling that had brought Lorna to Yrynn's lodge the first time and how they had met. Yrynn had simply been whispering the stories to herself. She had become so frustrated that she couldn't remember the true name of Little Blue that she'd growled deeply and smacked the bed with her broad tail. It was that smack that had stirred the bones, had made her notice this mist for the first time.

"Go on. Please . . . I do so love stories. . . ." That first time had been just a moon cycle ago, during the Month of the Tender Bark. It was a voice she had never before heard. It was Lorna.

In the beginning Yrynn could not quite see Lorna, for she had appeared as a mist, but soon odd shapes began to melt out of the mist and assemble themselves into a configuration. Yrynn realized those odd shapes were bones and that she was looking at a two-legs. Indeed a young girl. "I love your stories," Lorna had said that first time. "I've been listening to them for a long time."

"You have?"

"Yes, indeed. You are a great storyteller."

"I am?"

They had met many times since, and now Lorna was back again. So Yrynn began another story about when Little Blue fell from the sky into the sea. She whispered the words into the mist that seemed always to accompany Lorna at the end of her bed. An invisible wind stirred the tattered dress, and there was the dry sound of bones settling. So Yrynn began her story again, "Once, long ago in a far faraway land called Canada, a little star twinkled high, high in the sky. . . ."

When she had finished Yrynn turned to Lorna. "So you'll come back tomorrow, Lorna?"

"Yes." The little ghost nodded. "And maybe then you'll remember Little Blue's name."

"Maybe. But it seems so long ago that my mother told me that story. I wish I could remember the pup's name." She sighed. "But you said you had something to tell me. Something very important."

"Indeed, but . . . but it might scare you. . . . I'd like for my brother, Fergus, to come with me. But you know he's very shy."

"Oh, tell him I'm shy too," Yrynn replied.

"I suppose I could go try and fetch him now."

Yrynn peeped up through the cracks between the branches that formed the dome of her lodge.

"I think it's too late. It's long past dawn and our classes begin soon. The grown-ups are back from their Chomps and rested. I'm due at Was Meadow for Intermediate Wattling soon." She gritted her teeth and growled. "I hate that class!"

"Why?" Lorna asked.

Yrynn sighed. "Never mind," she said wearily.

The mist began to stir in the lodge. And slowly the bones dissolved back into the damp fog.

CHAPTER 8

Two Ghosts
Have a Spat

"*Fergus ... Fergus?*" *Lorna called out in the thickening mists of the feasghair.*

"Over here, Lorna. Turn at the old graveyard, the one by the church."

"What are you doing there?"

"You know the stone was put there. It was in the crypt of the church, if it's anyplace. But the crypt is all topsy-turvy. Everything is upside down there."

"Exactly, Fergus, honestly. We're in feasghair. Everything is upside down everywhere. That after all is what feasghair means in the old language—upside down, in between here and nowhere. Not heaven and not hell." Lorna spat out the words.

Fergus sighed. "But we're definitely dead. We're dead all right."

"Dead and homeless." Lorna's voice broke into a sob.

"Try not to cry, Lorna."

"How can I not cry? How come you aren't crying? Every year we spend here, every day in feasghair, I feel farther and farther from where we should rightfully be—in Neamorra."

"Well, did Yrynn say she'd help us look for the coronation stone?"

"I didn't ask."

"Well, why not?" Fergus said. An exasperated tone had crept into his voice.

"Fergus, I want you to come with me."

"No! You know what happened when we both went into that lodge of that one beaver kit."

"Dunwattle?"

"Yes, that one. He totally panicked, and that's why I lost my nerve."

"But I need you, Fergus. I can't explain it all on my own. How do I explain Neamorra? I don't know if beavers even have a heaven or what it's called. How do I explain the Coronation Stone, the Stone of Destiny, and how we shall be doomed to this cursed place forever if we don't find that stone? You tell me?"

"Don't blame me," Fergus said. The remnants of his thin pale hair rose from his skull. Two dim flames were beginning to glower in his eye sockets. Her brother did have a temper. "You know, Lorna, before the earthquake I thought I was really on the track of the stone, but since then, everything is topsy-turvy. But we did manage to find our bones, didn't we?"

"Fergus, we had found most of those bones over two centuries or so."

"But look, just the other day, we found some of Adair's. That's progress."

Lorna sniffed. She couldn't bear the thought of her adorable baby sister who had lived less than two years before she'd been murdered in the massacre.

"Fergus, it's not progress. Not really. We have to find the stone. Look, the stone has two names—the Coronation Stone and the Stone of Destiny—the second is its true name. Destiny, not just a king's or queen's destiny but ours. We belong in heaven, Neamorra. We lost Scotland to that evil English king, Longshanks. He took our village, and our lives, but we can't lose our chance for heaven. You must come with me Fergus, to meet Yrynn. I am telling you she is a very smart beaver. If any beaver in this pond, this pond where our village once stood, can help us, it's Yrynn. In a funny way, she is like us. She doesn't quite belong. And neither do we. We need to reach Neamorra, or the Belong."

"But she's alive and not dead, Lorna."

"That doesn't matter. I think . . . I feel . . ." *How to explain this?* Lorna thought. "I think she is a spirit of some sort. And although it makes her quite wonderful, it also makes her not quite belong to this place. They call her a Canuck. I'm not sure what that word means, exactly. Maybe different. Maybe not like the others. Maybe it means not to belong."

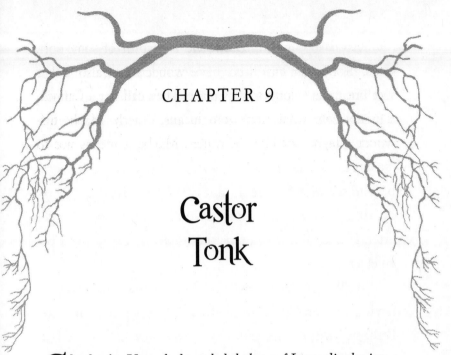

CHAPTER 9

Castor Tonk

Shortly after Yrynn had watched the bones of Lorna dissolve into a mist, she crawled out of her den and swam toward the muddy banks of Was Meadow. Other young kits were gathering where Castor Tonk had assembled three small heaps of mud alongside a stack of wattling branches and twigs. Tonk looked up and inhaled sharply as her eyes fell upon Yrynn clambering up on the bank between Dunwattle and Locksley.

"What are you doing here?" the teacher asked.

"I've been in intermediate since last fall. Castor Wanda promoted me just before . . . before she was murdered."

Tonk rolled her eyes toward the sky and muttered something incomprehensible.

"Alas, I suppose I must live with my predecessor's decisions." She gave a stiff little grimace that revealed only her small rear teeth but not her front incisors. It was considered a mildly offensive gesture not to reveal her bright orange working teeth. "We'll see if you're up to it."

Locksley slid his eyes toward Dunwattle. He did not need to say what he was thinking. *What an SBB!* Soggy bag of bark. This was the supreme insult that a beaver could utter. If a kit did this, he or she might be tail slapped by an elder.

"We'll begin class now," Castor Tonk intoned, "by identifying the three types of mud I have dug up to show you. Perhaps, Yrynn, since you have been in the class since last autumn, you might enlighten us?"

"I can try," Yrynn said meekly.

"Do try, please," Tonk rasped.

"I believe that one"—Yrynn pointed at the first pile—"is known as Old Red, and the one next to it with the gray pebbles in it is known as scrapple, and the third pile is called scripple."

"And what might be the differences between scrapple and scripple?" Castor Tonk asked.

"I . . . I . . ."

"Don't stammer, kit; out with it."

"I'm not sure," Yrynn blurted.

"Not sure?" Tonk opened her eyes wide. "My goodness,

I can't imagine why Castor Wanda would have promoted you to this level if you were not sure of the subtle differences among these three most basic types of mud. They're used in wattling all sorts of structures, from dams to lodges. And for our very important *stordahts* for storing wood during winter."

Dunwattle spoke up. "I don't know either, Castor Tonk, and Wanda was my grandmother!"

"Dunwattle! One does not speak without raising one's paw."

"Sorry."

"I should think you would be a bit ashamed of not knowing since—as you have just said—Castor Wanda was your grandmother, and a more noble Castor never lived." She tipped her head toward the sky and closed her eyes. It gave Dunwattle a strange sensation that beavers often called the *billies*, a cross between nausea and fear. It felt as if something was definitely off in the wood they were eating.

"I'm not ashamed," Dunwattle whispered under his breath.

Castor Tonk continued. "This term, we shall be covering the basic mud types and where they may be found. Many can be harvested right here in Was Meadow. So that is why we hold our first classes in this region of the pond. By end of term we shall move over toward New Fosters, where our esteemed Grand Aquarius lives. There we shall

examine the enriched variety of red mud so basic to dams."
Then she looked about.

"Now I would like you to choose a partner. Each of you shall take three dives and try to find a sample of these three kinds of mud for wattling."

Dunwattle and Locksley partnered with each other. But Yrynn was left sitting alone on the bank.

"Yrynn, you want to come with us?" Locksley said.

"Oh, I don't think that's a good idea at all," Castor Tonk replied.

"How come?" Dunwattle asked.

Tonk scowled. "Do you always question your elders in such a manner?" She did not wait for an answer. "Seeing as this Canu . . ." She stopped and began again. "Seeing as Yrynn is supposedly the most advanced in the class because of her early, and I hope not premature, promotion, I think she is perfectly capable of finding her own mud." She paused and swept her eyes toward Yrynn. "Are you not?"

"Yes, Castor Tonk." Yrynn instantly ducked under the water.

The class lasted a long time. And after wattling, they were to report to hydrology with Castor Elwyn. And after hydrology, there was a call for all kits to report to Dam 4, as there was a break threatening and help was needed in gathering reinforcement twigs from the west bank.

"Nothing like learning by doing!" Castor Elwyn

appeared ecstatic about this opportunity. The fur of Castor Elwyn's muzzle had faded with age to a pale creamy color, but there was never a more spry beaver. Quick of wit and deft of paws, he was a cheerful fellow and the best teacher of the pond. "A valuable moment we have here at Dam Four!" he called out. "It's a small leak, but they're the best for learning. You can't be slapdash. Delicate work, it is, and your tiny paws will be better at it than our big ole cloppers." As he swam, he turned his head back at the kits. "By the way, do you realize that our tiny front paws are the closest we get to what the two-legs call 'hands'?" A shiver went through Dunwattle. He had seen those hands—they flashed light, blinding white light. "Yes, our fingers are long and nimble—because we, like two-legs, have a first finger that can pivot to face our second. Hence, we can grasp things. Pinch the skinniest of twigs or pick up a nice rock to jam a leak." Castor Elwyn sighed. "How about that? Aren't we the greatest!"

They would work on Dam 4 until early in the evening. They had turned out to be the best hours of the first term day. For Castor Elwyn was an excellent teacher. And in Dunwattle's and Locksley's minds, the very best part of that day was when he spoke sharply to Retta, Tizia, and Gorsa for cutting off Yrynn. The three of them made what was known as a foul dive, to block Yrynn for a patch of mud that she had already claimed.

"Nope, not fair kits. Foul dive if I've ever seen one. I'm going to break up your merry little trio if you try that again!" Castor Elwyn had scolded.

There is some justice in this pond after all, Dunwattle thought as he heard Elwyn bellow at the dreadful trio.

By the time class was over, both Dunwattle and Locksley spied the shadows of the great wings of Elsinore printed on the pond, now silvered by moonlight.

"We're too late to tell her!" Locksley whispered. "She's gone on her flyover."

Dunwattle was relieved. His secret shame was locked within him. Couldn't he wait a bit longer for his grave misdeed to be revealed to the First Swan of Glendunny pond?

CHAPTER 10

In the Time
of the Glimmering

The last of the fireflies still hung in the air, flashing their secret language to one another. But those flashes would soon dissolve into the deep blue of the summer evening. The nights had grown shorter, the days longer and warming. It was the time between the winter and the summer solstice. The Castors called it *Misselthwith*. The Swans called it the Glimmering, for it was when the first tips of Cygnus, the summer constellation of the Swan, might be glimpsed. The nights of the Glimmering were Elsinore's time, or rather her excuse, for extensive surveillance flights, or flyovers, as swans called them. She would assess other ponds, new ponds, perhaps. The health of the weeds that flourished or perhaps didn't flourish. She would scout for willow groves, so necessary to the beavers' diet. But always she would also keep a sharp eye out for any nearby two-legs activity that threatened incursions. And she would try to scavenge for bits and pieces to please the G. A., and for herself the possibility of a book. She loved to read but would also bring back books for Kukla the librarian.

She had left the pond long before the night was over and flown due east and then south. There had been a tail feather wind, so she was able to fly above her normal cruising speed of thirty leagues per hour. Looking down, she now concluded that she was doing closer to forty. It was just after midnight when the moon began to slide west into another day. Then in the east she caught the first dim light of that distant constellation Cygnus. The tip stars were just ascending, hovering above the horizon. Of course, the constellation would not be visible for long. For on this shortened night it would soon be morning again, and the world would be bleached before the constellation reached its highest point. But for now, there would be at least a few hours when the swan stars would glimmer quietly, sublimely, in the awesome silence of the night. She swept high into the air to greet each star as it appeared. She played a game, one she had played with her mother, where she would swoop high into the summer night and greet each star one by one as it appeared to make the constellation. She had learned all their names from the song her mother had taught her. Now as she swept high into the darkness of the night, she sought that first star, Deneb, of the sky swan. . . . Ahh, there it was!

> *Hello, Deneb, my old friend*
> *I come to greet you once again*
> *I saw you sliding up, from afar tonight*
> *And just behind you Delta's pale pure light*
> *And now comes Albireo, shining in the wind*
> *Yet another old friend*
> *Within the silence of this night*
> *Through the stars I roam*
> *Listening to your lost songs alone*
> *I beg the day to wait*
> *And let other stars through the darkness of this gate*
> *Of a night so sublime*
> *If I could only halt time*
> *In the starry silence of this night*
> *I see a world at peace, no fools in sight*
> *Beneath your wings I shall glide*
> *Mute like my kind*
> *Till the night subsides.*

As she flew over Dam 4, she heard the words "What a genius!" float up and a round of applause as ten or more beavers began slapping their tails. It had to be applause for

Snert, a brilliant dam engineer. And her thought was quickly confirmed. "Snert does it again!" someone exclaimed. She looked down and saw the elderly beaver bowing his head as he accepted the ovation. From his posture he appeared humble, yet there was something so blatant in this display that it seemed as if he was anything but humble. He appeared to have perfected these postures. It was perhaps because of his facial disfigurement that he assumed these modest poses. It was almost as if he felt he could not really be so worthy—a beaver as different as he was. Snert had never been shunned by the pond inhabitants, but still, he was a most solitary creature. And nevertheless, he had steadily risen in the council of the Castorium.

Within a few hours after passing over Dam 4, Elsinore had crossed the Scottish border. Then in another hour she caught sight of the spires of Westminster Abbey. She skimmed over the spires just for fun and thought about all the dead kings and queens buried there, all the poets and scientists. It seemed rather sad to Elsinore that a two-legs, like a king or queen, already knew where he or she would be buried. She'd better not mention this to His Eagerness, or before she knew it, that ridiculous beaver would be trying to squeeze his way into a royal crypt in the Abbey!

Elsinore now angled her wings just a sliver and began to follow the sinuous black ribbon of a river—the River

Thames. It was just a short distance, perhaps a quarter hour at most, to one of her favorite spots: Richmond Palace. The palace was upstream, on the opposite bank of the Thames from Westminster Abbey.

There were unimaginable varieties of waterweeds in the sloughs, ditches, and side channels of the River Thames. The water in this region was thick with delicious weeds, including her favorite, water lettuce, along with Queensland mint clover. *And oh, be still my heart,* she thought, *and calm my gizzard at the mere notion of purple Salvinia.* She looked down at her foot and adjusted the ring. The last thing she wanted was to be tracked again by those idiots of the queen. The queen had many titles: the Defender of the Faith, the Sovereign of the Most Ancient and Most Noble Order of the Thistle, and last but most annoying, the Seigneur of the Swans. Elsinore recalled her conversation with the G. A. on this subject. *Imagine me addressing him as that. Not this swan!* Elsinore harrumphed and staggered slightly in her flight.

A few hours before dawn, long after the rising stars of Cygnus had slipped away into the thin filmy remnants of the last of the night, Elsinore glided into a sleepy backwater that bordered a pub. It was still early, so the pub was not yet bustling with people, or swans, for that matter. They often drifted by to be photographed or receive scraps of bread tossed by the customers on the terrace, who would begin arriving toward noon for lunch and a glass of ale. *Lazy old things, those pub swans*, Elsinore thought. Why go for a crust of bread already pecked by a two-legs, and ignore the succulent waterweeds so nearby? Preening their feathers, the swans would soon flock here to strike poses for the two-legs with their devices for making pictures.

Now, just as Elsinore was thinking of those picture-taking devices of the two-legs, a scrap of newspaper drifted by with a rather startling headline. She gasped.

WILD BEAVER SIGHTED FOR FIRST TIME IN 500 YEARS

Her gizzard went all squishy. The headline seemed to scream at her as she seized the paper in her beak and nearly shrieked, which is hard for a mute swan to do. But there was Dunwattle—clear as day. His little face and blinking eyes on the very front page of the newspaper. And that narrow tail, the Mumpsluff tail, the signature tail of that family cutting its distinctive wake behind him as he swam toward the banks of some river.

Her last thought was . . . Well, she was not sure, as she seemed to have fainted in a patch of water parsley.

And during that same approaching dawn, Yrynn now watched as the bones knitted together yet again into the shape she was growing to know so well.

"Lorna?"

"Yes, Yrynn. It's me. Well, sort of me. A ghost of me."

"That . . . that's all right. But where's your brother, Fergus? I thought you were going to try and bring him this time."

"Oh, you know Fergus. So shy."

"Was he always this shy?"

"You mean when he was alive? Before he was a ghost?"

"Yes," Yrynn replied.

"I think so but more so now. He has to get used to being . . . being dead, you know."

Yrynn was not sure how someone could get used to being dead.

"Being a ghost is slightly better than being dead, isn't it?"

Lorna seemed to hesitate. "We'll see." She sounded vague and seemed to look around. Yrynn watched her eyes, which were becoming clearer as her body took shape and became more defined in the dim light of the lodge. What did she mean by those words *We'll see?*

"I don't understand. Haven't you always been a ghost?"

"Oh no, not at all. Only since the earthquake."

"But that was just a few moons ago. So, what were you before?"

"Dead. Just plain dead."

"But when did you die?"

"All I know is that I never had my tenth birthday. I think it was only two days away when I died."

"You missed your first double-digit birthday!" Yrynn was shocked.

"What are digits?"

"Figures, numbers. You know like one-two-three-four-five-six-seven-eight-nine—"

"Ten yes, stop." Lorna held up her boney hand. Yrynn could see every joint in her finger bones.

"Of course, that was thoughtless of me. I didn't mean to rub it in."

"Oh no. Not thoughtless. How old are you?"

"Just two. But you know, beavers mature faster than two-legs."

"I'm a two-legs, right? Human."

"Uh . . . yes, I guess so."

"So if you're just two and mature faster than me, how old would that make you?"

Yrynn scratched her ear with a paw. "I suppose maybe eight or nine. Let me try and calculate. I'm very good with math—figures and all."

"You are?" Lorna said with sudden interest.

"Yes, Castor Feltch, who teaches scumology, has me count the pond blooms, the different kinds of waterweed, and mark down the dates they blossom and then wilt just before the ice comes. She says I am the most accurate counter. Even better than the grown-ups."

"I see. . . ." Lorna spoke slowly and scratched her own

ear, just a puffy little pink thing curled like a snail, perhaps, a snail out of its shell. Her finger went right through the ear, seemingly into her somewhat transparent head. *Don't spill your brains*, Yrynn wanted to say. "That's very interesting," Lorna whispered.

"Why? Do you have some scum, some pondweed you want me to count, Lorna?"

"No, but you could figure out how long I've been dead."

"I could?"

"Yes. You see, I was murdered two days before my birthday."

"Murdered! You were murdered?" Yrynn staggered slightly. "You mean you didn't die of . . . of . . . of a natural cause like sickness or something?"

"No. A most unnatural cause. Let's see. . . ." She paused. "My murder date was on which day of the week . . . ?" She lifted her fingers—they were sheer, almost translucent, and seemed to be counting. "I think I've got it. My birthday would have been a Tuesday, and the Massacre was the Friday before Easter Sunday. The year was 1296."

"1296!" Yrynn exclaimed. "You're almost a thousand years old."

"Not really. Remember, I'm dead."

CHAPTER 11

The Indignities of Death

"**B**limey, *think we got a dead one here, Percy. Yep, dead swan in the* weeds."

"Poor devil," another voice with a thick brogue muttered.

The voices sounded dim, as if coming from far away. Elsinore with her head beneath the broad fronds of a water hyacinth stirred. *What? Dead?* She was furious. She squawked and ripped up through the carpet of fronds.

"Good grief!" a bewhiskered man in black pants and the red vest of a waiter exclaimed.

The mute swan now put her vocal cords to work. *"Blyphynnphygg oggis larkschpileen grop."* Which in Old Swan, the language of Elsinore's forebearers, meant, "Go suck worms, you grievous morons." She was far from dead and her resentment boiled in her gizzard.

She spread her gorgeous white wings and lifted into the air, leaving the two men muttering as they watched her dissolve into a stack of clouds. Dawn had just broken. The sun glowed red beneath strata of long dark, sharklike clouds that swam just above the horizon. From Elsinore's vantage point, it appeared as if the rim of the earth had caught fire. She was beating against a headwind, but nothing would deter her. She had to get back to Glendunny. Back to her nest on the pond. And most important, she had to confront Dunwattle. Where had he been exactly? And what had he done to come to the attention of a two-legs with a picture machine—what did they call those things? Cameras! Yes, that was the word. Elsinore's mind was a muddle. She rose higher in the sky, slipping the skin of the earth, flying as hard and fast as she could. She knew that she had to get away, get away and get beyond it in order to think. She powered up and rose into an even higher stratum in the cumulous mass of clouds as England dissolved beneath her.

By the time she was over Scotland and beginning her descent, she felt the thick, damp mist of the moors engulfing her. It was soothing. Once in her nest she needed to sleep, sleep in order to think. It was a swan habit. By twisting her neck and tucking her head beneath her wing, with her ear slit pressed against the rhythms of her heart, her mind would become one with her heart. It was not simply thinking—it was called "sorting." She would sort things out in her mind and figure out how to deal with this absolutely catastrophic event of Dunwattle's sighting.

She was unsure why this time-honored posture aided thinking and the activity of her brain. Her great-grandfather many times over Alastair had theorized that it was because of the multitude of feathers that grew around the head and neck of a swan. Every swan had more than twenty-five thousand feathers. The majority of these feathers crowded around their heads and neck. Counting feathers had been her great-grandfather's lifelong project. He had estimated that the average number that grew around a swan's head and neck was at least eighteen thousand. These were exceptionally small, almost miniscule feathers that he speculated assisted brain activity as they quivered during *schwanka,* a special swan sleep state in which higher thinking could occur. She needed hours of undisturbed sleep, of schwanka! To ensure that she would get this deep sleep, Elsinore raised her Do Not Disturb sign. It was a flag she had woven herself from cattails. If the fuzzy parts of the cattails were upside down, she meant, "Don't you dare disturb me!" Even the Grand Aquarius observed the cattail flag.

She had been asleep, in a state of deep schwanka, for close to an hour. She seemed to be just on the brink of determining where exactly the disastrous occurrence had happened. And at the same time, she was trying to figure out an escape route for the foolish Dunwattle—for all of the beavers, for that matter. Nowadays the two-legs did not have such a penchant for beaver hats, but they still hated the beavers for flooding their precious landscape where they wanted to build large mansions or farms or their outrageous theme parks!

What of course the two-legs did not realize is that their precious land would be entirely worthless if the water table was not maintained. If water-storing wetlands disappeared, farmers would not be able to farm, and species of birds and insects would simply vanish as well. Water meant life. Water shaped continents, and the beavers were the builders of these continents through their meticulous maintenance of the water table and their creation of ponds like the one in Glendunny.

Elsinore began to stir in her sleep. Yes, the beavers of Glendunny were more important to Scotland than any king or queen. Beavers were a keystone species—what very few two-legs realized. And what was a keystone? The central stone in an arch that locked everything together so it wouldn't fall apart. But it wasn't simply a building in this case. It was the earth! But no one knew this or appreciated beavers for what they were. Particularly in England, as no one had seen a beaver for centuries. The Castors of Glendunny were the biggest secret on earth. The secrets of the universe and those of the most distant stars were perhaps more reachable than those of Glendunny.

Through the fraying veils of Elsinore's deep sleep, she heard the low voices of kits squabbling at the base of the G. A.'s lodge.

"We can't wake her up, Locksley. Her flag is flying. Even the G. A. doesn't disturb her when it's hoisted."

"This is no ordinary situation, Dunwattle. She has to know. What you've done is . . . is . . . I can't even think of a word."

"Yes you can!" A voice hissed from above. Both beavers felt those pouches in their deep gut, their skeats, roil with gaseous bubbles of undigested bark.

"Meet me at the styg," Elsinore whispered down from her perch.

The *styg* was what swans often called their ground nest, the place where they tended their baby swans, cygnets. It was away from the pond, where she held her most private conversations. Water carried sound too easily. Elsinore's styg was a shapely bowl made of sedges and other water plants that she had ripped up, built on the abandoned den of a muskrat. She had no cygnets, but she enjoyed the privacy of the place, where she could talk and counsel young beavers. Despite the fact that kits were an entirely different species from herself, she treated them as she would if they had been her very own cygnets. She soothed them by running her beak through their stiff fur and listening to them attentively. The kits trusted her, but she could be severe when necessary.

"You know?" Dunwattle gasped. His eyes filled with tears. He began to shake with shame. "You know that I—" Elsinore cut him off. "Don't say the word." The V word of course. "How did this happen?"

Locksley gave Dunwattle a sharp glance. No words were needed. Dunwattle knew what he was warning. *Don't leave anything out. Bones, ghosts, and all!* But how did Elsinore know that he had been seen?

Despite their caution, however, despite the absence of uttering the word "vysculf," and despite their low voices, there was another set of ears listening. Those ears picked up just enough to know that a sacred dictum handed down centuries ago by the Castorium had been violated. And that dictum was the vysculf. The law forbidding beavers to be seen by any two-legs.

And those ears didn't belong to another beaver but to a lynx. Not just any lynx but Grinfyll, the leader of the most vicious of the assassination curses. Normally curses were comprised of ten or a dozen lynx. But Grinfyll's curse of killer lynx was elite. Only eight were ever selected, no matter the size of their prey.

Those eight lynx had the power of two dozen. All lynx

were not only swift and efficient killers with the sharpest teeth and claws of any creature in the forest of Glendunny, but they also had the sharpest ears. They could detect a mouse from a great distance, perhaps a quarter of a league away. Grinfyll tried to listen more closely. Was it one of these two beavers who had been seen? What were their names now? That was always the problem, for as smart and strategic as lynx were about killing, they were rather stupid in other ways. It was as if they were designed to do just that one thing: kill. They were poor in language skills. And they couldn't remember a name if their lives depended on it. They could remember other aspects—their scent, their manner of walking or swimming, of barking or squealing or yelping—but not their names. Perhaps they could keep a name in mind for a few fleeting minutes, but after that the name just dissolved into the fog of their brains. So they often just settled on a letter sound, and that became the name for a while. No multisyllable sounds or names could cling to their brains. And he knew that these two kits had just such multisyllable names.

But certainly it could not be either one of these two kits who had been seen. They didn't seem to have the where-withal to travel the distance to where one of them might encounter a two-legs. Grinfyll wished he could creep closer, but the wind had just shifted and that would bring his scent closer to them. Beavers had very keen senses of smell.

But that gave him another idea. X! Ah yes, his old friend X! Another creature whose name he could never quite remember.

X was a greedy old soul and a distinguished member of the Castorium. He felt that he had been passed over to become the Aquarius, denied his place in the line of succession—the Avalinda line of royal succession. W had been elected over him. So X had come to Grinfyll to—as he put it—"see if things could be arranged." In short, the assassination of W. . . . Now what had W stood for? Of course. The name exploded in Grinfyll's head. Wanda the Wattler! It was always so exciting when an entire name came back to him. In some mysterious way it lifted his spirits. It made him almost believe that he could become more than a killer, if he truly had language.

X had always assumed that he himself would be the next in line. The runner-up. But he wasn't. So Grinfyll had helped him out with the very efficient murder of Wanda. And X himself was certain that after Wanda he must have had the most votes. There was no way of knowing for sure, but he was certainly smarter than the current Aquarius, Oscar of Was Meadow. He had done more for the pond. But at the same time, he was much older than Oscar. And that was what the beavers of the Castorium must have thought. A perhaps weaker but younger Aquarius would serve the pond better. X was shocked when the announcement was made. He could think only that they felt he was too old and that Oscar could learn, could grow into the task.

But younger was not always better. Oscar had proven this already, and it was a complete surprise when this rather wimpish idiot came to rule. Two murders in a row would not be tolerated. X himself had no one to complain to except Grinfyll, who listened. At the same time, although he complained to the lynx, he nevertheless treated him with contempt. And this disturbed Grinfyll profoundly. X once called him "thuggish." It nettled the lynx to no end. Grinfyll even offered to kill the new Aquarius. "Stupid moron," X had thundered at the lynx. "You think they won't become suspicious?" "Huh?" was all Grinfyll could answer, but inside he was withering. He couldn't stand the way X treated him. And yet he was drawn to him. He felt somehow that X could empower him. He secretly knew that all lynx were regarded as thugs. And he wanted more out of life. He once said to his sister, "All we do really well is kill. Our brains are simple compared to the brains of the rest of the animals of Glendunny. Even fireflies are better than we are, with their complicated language of flashes. No creature really respects us."

"You can't eat respect," his sister had replied. In the same instant she shot out and pounced on a little family of moles that had just emerged from a small hole. She swallowed all of them at once. He could see the bulge in her throat as they went down. Then giving a slight burp, she sighed. "Can't beat that, can you? Six in one blow. Tasty little fellas. Bones and all."

Actually, Grinfyll felt he could almost taste respect. And now he had information that was extremely valuable to X and his craving for power. It wasn't Grinfyll's fault that Oscar of Was Meadow was the Aquarius. Who could have known that the Castorium council would have chosen *him* as a successor to Wanda? But now they were disenchanted with this very vain beaver. And how much more disenchanted would they be to learn that their most sacred law, vysculf, had been violated on this Aquarius's watch? If X could be the hero in this situation . . . well, the lynx mused, things might change. And it all might work out well for Grinfyll. He wanted so little, really—just respect.

All he really wanted to say to X was *You don't gotta love me, but you gotta respect me.* But of course, he didn't have the nerve. He had the nerve to kill, but not the nerve to ask for what he genuinely deserved. He thought he might get respect when he led the curse to kill Wanda. At that point he thought one could perhaps eat respect. And Wanda the Wattler was more than just respected. There was another word he had heard some creatures say about Wanda, but he often forgot it. What was it? He searched his tiny mind. *Esteemed!* That was the word. Yes, she was respected and *esteemed.* Wanda was not a thug. And he had killed her.

Those hoity-toity beavers of the pond thought lynx were simply predators. They were fearful of the lynx, wary of their elite killing teams—the curses. He was sick and tired when he thought of all the times he had heard the beavers call lynx thugs. Wanda herself had called him a thug with her dying breath! Spat it out right in his face. And he had seen a strange light in her misty eyes in those last seconds as she lay dying—a smirk. That beaver actually had the audacity to smirk at her killer. It was as if she were saying, *You are nothing. You only kill. But we . . .* And then as she was choking, she had said out loud, "We build. We beavers change the world. We have built continents. . . ." And Grinfyll's last words to her were "You disrespect me!" and then he bit deeper into her neck.

But Wanda's words had haunted him ever since. Haunted him so much that he could now remember her full name without half trying. She was Wanda the Wattler, who had called him a thug! All he had ever craved was respect. Now there was a chance for him to gain that at last. He must visit X, for he knew that a beaver had now been seen by a two-legs. The rule of V, vysculf—the word exploded in his mind. Yes, that rule had been violated! Grinfyll didn't need to hear anymore. He must send a signal to X immediately. The information he had was valuable indeed.

CHAPTER 12

A Most Dreadful Story

The lynx should not have been in such a hurry. *Had Grinfyll* stayed, he would have learned more. But he had rushed off, just as Elsinore began to tell the kits another tale. Then again, language was always difficult for lynx. Other animals spoke in such long winding syllables and big complicated words. He'd heard all he needed.

"It's a long story and a dreadful story," Elsinore began. "It's a story too shocking for young ears. But I have no choice, as it's one you must hear. Then you will understand how dangerous it is that you have been seen." The swan looked directly into Dunwattle's eyes. The young kit felt that ghastly squishiness once more in his skeat.

"Now mind you. No other beavers except for those

members of the Castorium know this story. They are told it upon their admission to the council." Elsinore looked at them steadily and then began. "You see, once upon a time—a very long time ago—more than five hundred years ago—there was a king. He was a great and powerful king. He was called Henry the Eighth."

"Why the Eighth?" Locksley asked.

"Because there had been seven Henrys before him," Elsinore snapped. "Try not to interrupt, dear."

"Henry had a hunting lodge. It was called Great Fosters and was far to the south of Glendunny. And New Fosters, the Aquarius's lodge, is named for that place where the king liked to hunt."

"Hunt?" Dunwattle asked.

Oh dear, the swan thought. This was going to be difficult. She looked at the two young beavers now and thought how innocent they were. To a creature that only gnawed wood to eat and build, the concept of killing a living thing was completely strange—even alien. "Hunting is what two-legs do when they get hungry for meat."

"They're like lynx," Locksley said. "They kill?"

"Well, yes, I suppose so."

"But this two-legs I saw looked nothing like a lynx. Not the beady eyes or snout. No beak like an owl. I mean, honestly, it didn't look as if it could kill a thing."

"Well, they do." Elsinore sniffed. "And not only do they

hunt for the meat, but they love the fur. So they skin the beavers for it."

"What?" Both kits gasped and gripped their own pelts.

"Yes, they skin the beavers. They love the fur and it keeps them warm."

At that moment Dunwattle threw up a pile of half-digested spruce.

"Oh, you poor dear. I didn't mean to alarm you, but there is no gentle way to explain this, the ways of humans."

Dunwattle was now moaning. "I didn't mean to mess up your nest," he said, looking at the pile of undigested bark.

"No matter, I can get fresh reeds. But you need to hear this story, and it only gets worse, I'm afraid."

"Go on," Locksley said weakly.

"Well, the Aquarius of the pond at Great Fosters back then—Avalinda—decided that they all had had enough of King Henry—'Big Hank,' they called him. Their numbers were dwindling. So they set out to find a new place to live, to create a pond that was so remote that no one would ever find it. Avalinda, with the guidance of First Swan, headed north. However, a splinter group of beavers headed due west. Your ancestors were part of the northern group."

"Where did the others go?"

"That's another story for another time. But they crossed a vast sea to what was then called the New World to Canada, where the Canuck beavers come from. But this here is your world. The Old World. This island of ours contains both England and Scotland."

"This is an island?" Locksley asked, looking toward the mound of peat that formed a small island in their own pond. It would always rise higher when the water level dropped in the summer.

"It is many times vaster than Peat Island, believe me."

Locksley's mind was swirling with the unimaginable things, the fearful things that had come from Elsinore's beak in the last few minutes. "All right," he said softly. "Go on."

"Well," continued Elsinore. "Avalinda was one smart beaver, if there ever was one. She had decided that it was not good enough to find just a faraway, isolated place but a place that two-legs would dread to come near. She thought of the most northern part of the island, Scotland. You see, she knew many bloody wars had been fought there, two hundred years or so before the time of Big Hank. Perhaps she could find a place so cursed that two-legs would be frightened to come anywhere near it." Now Elsinore looked again at Dunwattle. The young beaver blinked. "I think you know why, dear Dunwattle?"

Dunwattle remained silent. Elsinore blinked and stretched out her wing as if to support him. "You saw the bones, didn't you?" Dunwattle dipped his head. "And you saw a . . . a . . ."

"Yes, the ghost . . . the one I first told you about . . . and . . . and bones. And she told me a most dreadful story." Dunwattle almost choked on the word. "You see, I didn't just see that ghost—and there might have even been two ghosts—but the one, she sat right down . . . as if she . . . she wanted to explain something."

"And you fled? That is how you came to be seen?" the swan said quietly.

"Yes," Dunwattle murmured in a low voice. Shame roiled through him.

"It was the earthquake three moons ago that must have disturbed all the bones," Elsinore said.

"All the bones?" Locksley asked.

"The bones of the bloodiest massacre in the history of this fair isle. That must be what the ghost wanted to explain to you—the story . . . the story of this village where she once lived." Elsinore took a deep breath. "You see . . ." For the second time she said, "Once upon a time."

She paused and seemed to swallow as if something were caught in her throat or neck, perhaps somewhere between the nineteenth and twenty-second vertebra of that very long neck, which had twenty-four of those little vertebra bones. "You see, there was a terrible king, long before Big Hank, much more bloodthirsty, if that can be imagined. He was called Edward Longshanks for his very long, exceptionally long legs. He'd come from England into Scotland to conquer it. But he didn't just conquer—he massacred the town of Glendunny."

"Massacred?" Dunwattle asked in a trembling voice.

"Slaughtered." She let the word hang in the air. What a terrible word. This was a word that sounded like what it was—blood drenched.

Elsinore continued. "It was said that for two days blood ran from the bodies of those murdered two-legs."

"But why? Why did he do this?" Locksley asked.

"Why? Why did this King Longshanks do it? Why do curses of lynx go out and kill things when they are not even hungry? Such creatures have appetites for more than just food. They crave power and they feed on the fear of others. It was written that in his tyrannical rage Edward Longshanks ordered seventy-five hundred two-legs massacred. There were rivers of blood!"

The two young beavers shivered.

"And . . . and . . ." Locksley tried to speak. "These were the bones that Dunwattle saw?"

Now Dunwattle began to speak in a barely audible voice. "There was more than just bones."

"What do you mean?" Locksley asked, and Elsinore herself looked puzzled.

How to explain this? Dunwattle thought. He was at a loss for words. He felt slightly out of his own body as he remembered awakening and seeing the figure at the end of his bed. It all became so real again, as if a veil were lifting. Those ghastly bones had melted out of the mists of his dreams—except he had not been dreaming. Those weren't merely dreams. He had been awake. And he had seen more than just bones—also the tattered bloodstained remnants of what the furless two-legs called clothing.

"The bones began to . . . well, sort themselves out. There was a two-legs but possibly another as well."

"You mean four legs in all?" Locksley said.

"Yes, two separate creatures," Dunwattle replied. "Four legs in all. One I believe was a girl, and one was a boy. Maybe sister and brother. And they wore clothing. Isn't that what they call it? Castor Helfenbunn taught us that in our Two-legs Vigilance lessons. So we could report if we'd seen one or found any clothes."

"We didn't pay much attention, though," Locksley said. "Hard to study for something you've never seen. Hard to believe they exist."

"But they do exist," Dunwattle said fiercely. "I've seen them both."

"Both? You mean the sister and the brother?" Locksley asked.

"No, I mean both dead and alive. The one with the flashing hands was alive. And the worst thing is that now I've been seen."

"By both?" Locksley's voice trembled.

"Yes, the girl bones—well, she looked right at me. The fur on her head, I mean the hair—remember Castor Helfenbunn said two-legs called that stuff that grows from their heads hair? It was red and her eyes were blue. Blue—can you believe it? Blue eyes, as if little bits of the sky had fallen into her face. I'm not sure about the other set of bones, her brother, maybe." He shut his own eyes tight, as if trying to recall the moment. "But she looked right at me. It was as if she dared me to look at her too."

"And did you?" Elsinore asked.

"No. I was too scared. I bolted out of the den and swam as hard as I could. I went over Dam Eight into the shunting canals and then into streams and followed them to a river."

"Good grief!" Elsinore clapped her bill closed in dismay. "And that's when you encountered the live human—a two-legs?"

Dunwattle slumped and nodded.

"And the two-legs took your picture, your photograph?"

"Is that what the flash was—the white light?" Dunwattle asked.

"Yes. They call it a photograph," Elsinore added, thinking of the picture on the newspaper that had blown into the canal by the pub.

"I'm going to have to leave, aren't I, Elsinore? If only that two-legs had been simply a ghost like the other one! Now I've been seen."

"Don't jump to conclusions. Not yet. Let's wait a bit. Let's let things settle."

Like the bones, both Dunwattle and Locksley thought. And yet they all knew that the bones of the dead weren't the problem. It was the living creature Dunwattle had seen on the riverbank. But what riverbank? What stream? There were hundreds, if not thousands of waterways between the pond and wherever it was that Dunwattle had fled to.

Meanwhile Locksley had been thinking very hard about the dreadful story and the terrible secret that Elsinore had revealed.

"You said that the Castorium knows about this terrible secret of the massacre?" Locksley asked.

"Yes, once one is elected to the Castorium, the secret is revealed. It was decided many years ago that the reason behind the rule of vysculf could be known only to the council." Elsinore took a deep breath. "I have always felt that was a wrong decision. Members of a community, of a pond such as ours, should know why they are expected to obey such a rule. Creatures, beavers in particular, are more willing to obey a rule or a law if they know the reason behind it."

"So, the council members are the only ones who know?" Locksley asked.

"Yes," Elsinore said hesitantly.

"Then how do you know?" the young kit pressed.

Dunwattle was suddenly alert. "Yes, how do you know Elsinore? You're not a member of the Castorium."

She drew herself up to her full height. "I am First Swan of this pond. I am a direct descendant of Byatta, who was First Swan at the pond of Great Fosters. Avalinda was the Aquarius, the leader of beavers of that pond. Who do you think found this pond for Avalinda? Who flew out on a stormy night right before King Henry's—Big Hank's—Michaelmas celebration?"

"Mik-a-what?" Dunwattle asked.

"Never mind that. Big Hank had a peculiar way of celebrating holidays. He liked to go hunting. Slaughter beavers. That was his idea of fun. But it was Byatta, the swan of the pond at Great Fosters, who found this place. And she was best friends with Avalinda."

"But I still don't understand. Why do you know or how do you know the secret?"

Elsinore took a deep breath. "The first swans ever since Byatta have always known this secret. It is in the *Cygnus*, the Book of Swan. Aquarius Avalinda thought that it was essential that the swans know this secret but that the future members of the Castorium not be aware that the swans knew. She worried that in the future we might have a weak Aquarius, as we do now, or perhaps traitors among the beavers within the Castorium." She paused for a long time. "And then of course we have other ways of learning things."

"What other ways?" Locksley asked.

Elsinore sighed. There was no use evading these questions, not when Dunwattle was in such danger. "We swans have superb auditory skills. We can hear through wood and wattle, mud and stones. We can hear you when you are deep in your lodges. It is the tradition of First Swans to build their nests in the center of things, atop the sprawling Aquarius's lodge, where the chambers of the Castorium are."

"And you can hear the Castors below?"

"Every word," she said sharply, then turned to Dunwattle.

"Dunwattle, dear, do you have any idea where you were when you were spied?"

"Not really."

"What was the water like?"

"Very clear. No pondweed, a bit of current in some places . . . but . . ." His voice dwindled. He was at a complete loss.

"Well," Elsinore chirped almost gaily. "In the meantime, we must carry on. Yes, keep calm and carry on!"

Carry on? How could they? both Dunwattle and Locksley thought. Especially after this horrendous, bloody story of a mad king and murder.

"You must go to classes as you usually do. Listen attentively. Learn what you can. I think a new assignment might be coming out today. You might be sent to work on Dam

Seven or help with shredding. The Grand Aquarius needs some new bark," Elsinore said.

"He always needs new bark for that throne of his."

"Now, now, Locksley. Kindly refrain from any criticism of your elders."

"But—"

"No buts, Locksley. As I said, act as if nothing has happened. Keep calm and carry on."

CHAPTER 13

"Go to
the Otters"

A massive old beaver in the lower reaches of the pond swam from his den toward a dilapidated dam not yet scheduled for repair. Three stripped willow branches had been affixed to the top of the dam as a sign for him by the lynx. It was a mark that no other beaver would recognize.

Now what does that lynx want? X thought. Of course he had another name. But the lynx had no memory for names, and he felt it best that Grinfyll called him simply X. The beaver clambered over the wreckage of the dam and followed a path through the woods into a grassy meadow.

As X approached, waddling through the high grasses, the lynx watched him from a thicket. Because of X's broad tail he cut a wide swath. He was one of those beavers that seemed to crave isolation. He rarely left his lodge or met up with other beavers.

When Grinfyll had asked the beaver what his name was he had merely replied, "I know more about your wee brain than you do. So no need to complicate things. Names, long words, language are not in your skill set. 'X' will do for you." *For you.* The two words scalded Grinfyll's ears, and he felt something wither inside him. It galled him to no end. He wasn't good with names, but he could try at least. It was as if the beaver was saying that Grinfyll did not deserve to address him by his real name. Or perhaps he wanted the lynx to beg him. Well, he wouldn't beg. But this time it would be different. X would relish what he was about to tell him.

The lynx drew himself up proudly as he stepped forward from a clump of hedges. His luminescent eyes glittered. He held his ears rigidly. He was so much more elegant than this squat, waddling creature with his flat tail and awkward gait. So what if the beaver had a silver streak down his back that flashed like a bolt of lightning through a furry sky. Perhaps this was considered a handsome marking on a beaver. Yet X's face could not be called handsome. A bulbous growth crawled across it, boiling up hideously. Was it a growth or a scar from some long-ago battle? Unlikely it was a battle, as beavers were not fighters. Perhaps a wound when a tree fell the wrong way in a sudden wind. His other eye, the one that was not obscured, glared with a mad light that glittered when he became deeply interested in something.

"I have news for you . . . news that could benefit you. . . ." Grinfyll hesitated. He wanted to see this beaver yearning, hoping—eager! But the beaver remained calm. He even had the audacity to yawn right in Grinfyll's face.

"And what might that be?" he muttered, his voice thick with boredom.

"The . . . the . . . the V word. I can't remember the whole word."

"V word," X replied lazily. "Now, you wouldn't mean *the* V word? Vysculf?"

"Yes! That's the one, that's the one!" The lynx gave a little leap into the air. He was so excited. "Vysculf! A young beaver has been seen by a two-legs."

X yawned again. "Where?"

"Where? How should I know where? I just know he's been seen," Grinfyll replied.

Now X tipped his head back, seemed to roll his beady eyes toward the sky. "How should you know?" he said. The words dripped with mockery.

"I don't understand?" Grinfyll was confused.

"Of course you don't, you dolt. Don't you realize it doesn't matter if a beaver was seen or not at this point? Nor does it even matter which beaver was seen. The crucial fact is where the beaver was seen in relation to the two-legs.

How close are the two-legs to us? That's what matters," X said disdainfully, then turned and began to leave.

"Wait! You can't leave now."

"And why, pray tell, can't I leave?" X replied as he continued through the high grass.

"W-w-w-well . . . how am I supposed to find out where this beaver was seen? Just how do I do that?" Grinfyll asked.

"Don't whine," X snapped. "I can't abide whiners. And what creature on earth has a better sense of smell than you?"

"Um . . . otters?" Grinfyll asked.

"Indeed. Go to the otters. They can sniff it out." Then X stopped. And turned around slowly. This gave Grinfyll some hope. "And by the way. A question for you, Grinfyll of Slanaigh. Yes, you once told me that was your full name. Can you still remember your own name?"

The lynx felt his heart skip a beat. X was calling him by his full name? Was this the first step toward that elusive respect that he craved?

"Yes, yes I can."

"Do you know what the word *slanaigh* even means?"

Grinfyll wished he'd never uttered the word to X. For suddenly the sound of that word coming out of X's proud, scornful mouth seemed to have a slight stench to it—as if to suggest that the lynx was too stupid to know the meaning of his own name.

"Uh . . . I think it's an old family name."

"It means 'soul,' you foolish creature. Soul, the trash you leave behind after you have picked the bones. But you wouldn't know a soul if it slapped you in the face." And with that he turned and slapped his broad tail on the ground.

Grinfyll felt disappointed, and yet the words that X had just spoken resonated. *What creature on earth has a better sense of smell than you? Go to the otters. . . .*

Well, he thought, *that is what I must do.* That would be simple. He must find an otter to help him, an otter with something to lose even larger than its own life. *Of course!* he thought. *A female with newborn pups! What could be better? He could threaten death to her newborn pups.* In the depraved mind of a lynx like Grinfyll, this would mean respect. He skipped off almost gaily as he began to imagine the respect that would soon be his.

CHAPTER 14

The Threat of the Lynx

"*Aren't they adorable?*" *The lynx cooed at the pups, which were just* hours old. It had taken him a day to find a mother otter with newborns. But now he had. It was a perfect family. No father evident. A widowed mum, so it seemed, as otters usually mated for life. "Now, what are their names?" Grinfyll asked.

Why is he here? Glory thought. Lynx and otters never mingled. Lynx were not river creatures at all. They were inferior swimmers at best. They shared no common interests in terms of food. Otters were fish eaters. Lynx liked red-blooded meat. But she dared not look at this lynx directly. She had heard about the strange transfixing light that could radiate from their eyes and render their victims helpless.

"Their names?"

"Yes, madame. Their names."

"Iglemore and Edlmyn."

How will I ever remember those! Grinfyll thought. "Odd names," he replied.

"Not really. You see, they were born between the rise of the two evening stars, Iglemore and his sister star, Edlmyn. But why do you need to know their names?"

"I always like to know the names of the creatures that I might eat."

The otter gasped. "What—what are you saying? That you might eat my pups?"

"Might!" Grinfyll said in a low voice. "You want them to grow up, to be strong, smart pups like their late father, undoubtedly?" Grinfyll purred.

"Undoubtedly," she whispered, her voice trembling.

"Well, then I have a little favor to ask of you."

Glory felt her heart almost stop, or at least skip several beats.

"So sad your mate couldn't live to see these two young'uns, but they could still join him."

Glory staggered a bit. She gripped the root that was poking through the floor of her den. This couldn't be happening. But it was.

The lynx continued to speak in that slimy voice. "A Castor has been seen by a two-legs. It is a violation of their most sacred law. It might be a young one who broke this law. I overheard a conversation between two kits and the swan. All these kits look alike to me. But they have different scents, and they carry the scent of waters—even waters that are strange to those of the pond. You, dear otter, as other otters, can pick up the scent of distant waters on a Castor. I know you can."

"It's very difficult," Glory said. Her normally sleek fur was standing up around her neck. A sure sign of terror.

"Well, that's your problem, dearie."

Now the lynx did something awful. He crouched low and peered at Iggy. There was a hungry gleam in his eye, and he whispered in a low, rough voice, "What a little cutie you are." Then he poked out his pale tongue and licked his lips. "And sweet too." It was at that moment that Glory collapsed in a faint. By the time she came to just a few seconds later Grinfyll was gone. But she knew he was not gone forever. He'd be back. She'd have no choice. She would not lose her pups. But why was it so important for the lynx to know where that beaver had been swimming? Why should a lynx care if a Castor had been seen? What was it to Grinfyll?

CHAPTER 15

Touched
by a Ghost

This must be a soul that I am seeing, Yrynn thought as she watched the bones now completely assembled and the tattered dress stirred by some invisible breeze. The soul of Lorna was smiling at her so, so sweetly. Souls knew no age. They were simply the pure, ageless essence of a once-living creature that endured beyond their years on earth.

"Hallo." Lorna smiled at Yrynn.

"Hallo, Lorna." Yrynn loved saying the little ghost's name. "You came back."

"Of course."

"But where is your brother, Fergus? Still shy?"

"Uh . . ." She seemed to hesitate. "Well, yes." Then the child began to shimmer. A pale blue glow appeared to radiate from her. It was the color of dusk, that moment at the end of twilight, just before the night sky sets in. "You see, Yrynn, we've been watching you. You seem to not be frightened off by us like Dunwattle. Good heavens, he just fell to pieces."

This seemed like an odd choice of words for a two-legs who just a short time ago was literally in pieces herself. She was amazed that Dunwattle had been approached by Lorna as well.

"You see, we have a secret and . . . Fergus doesn't think we should tell you. Or tell anybody." Lorna sighed softly.

Another secret? Weren't these bones secret enough? Yrynn thought.

"I told you about the murder."

Yrynn nodded. "You called it a massacre."

"Yes. A mass murder. I suppose that's where the phrase comes from."

Yrynn marveled at how calm Lorna seemed to be. But seeing as she had been dead for close to a thousand years, Yrynn supposed she had had time to grow accustomed to the idea. Lorna had said the massacre happened in the year 1296. Yrynn had done a quick calculation in her head—*717 years ago!*

But Lorna interrupted her calculations. "There is of course more to the story. King Edward who led the massacre—Edward the First—had a nickname."

"What?" Yrynn asked. "Edward the Bloody?"

"No, he was called Longshanks."

"Longshanks?"

"Yes, he was an extremely tall two-legs, as you call them."

"How do you know we call them two-legs. How?"

"Fergus and I often listen in on your classes. I believe it's Professor Helfenbunn who teaches TLV."

"Two-legs Vigilance—aspects and behavior of the enemy species. You listen to that? It's so boring."

"Depends on your perspective, I suppose. Hearing yourself described by a beaver is . . ." She hesitated. "Startling. But I believe you are an outstanding pupil."

"Well, not really." Yrynn bowed her head modestly.

"But you are! They just don't like to think that a Canuck Castor, a beaver from Canada, can be so smart. It's so unfair."

"Not fair at all! But how do you know all this?"

"Oh, we've learned a lot since the earthquake. Since our bones were unsettled. Fergus and I listen in all the time."

"How many of you, or how many bones have been unsettled?"

"We're not sure. So far we seem to be the only ones that came close to the surface."

"But this king, Longshanks?"

"Oh yes—him," Lorna replied. "Well, when Longshanks conquered our village and killed everyone, he also confiscated the Coronation Stone. Sometimes called the Stone of Destiny." Yrynn blinked, but remained silent. "Here's the thing. He thought he took this ancient-looking stone with some old carvings and symbols on it with him back to England. He believed it was the stone of the King of the Scots. But that king, King John Balliol, outsmarted Edward Longshanks. He had his stonecutters carve out and chisel another stone to look like it. But the real stone, the true stone, is still here . . . somewhere."

"Here? Here in this pond?"

"Indeed. Of course, during the time of the massacre, this wasn't a pond. It was a lively village. The fake stone had been dragged to King Balliol's castle where the real one would be expected, and the real one was put in our peasant village, where no one would ever expect it to be. I think that it was hidden in a blacksmith's forge. Others think it was buried in a graveyard or the crypt of the village church. So, Edward Longshanks took the fake one from Balliol's castle and carried it off to England. To Westminster Abbey. It now sits directly under a throne where every monarch—king or queen—has sat during their coronation."

"But they don't know it's a fake, not a real one?" Yrynn asked.

Lorna shook her head. Her skull glowed through the mist of her pale red hair. "No." She paused for a moment. "Who is the king right now?" Lorna asked.

"Uh . . ." Yrynn thought back to Helfenbunn's class. She should remember this. "Uh . . . well, actually it's a lady, a queen."

"Queen. Interesting," Lorna replied. "There haven't been many of those. Well, don't tell her. She might be very disappointed that she's been sitting on a fake Stone of Destiny and not the real one."

"I doubt she'd listen to a beaver. A Canuck one at that," Yrynn replied, and they both giggled.

"Yes, now I recall," Yrynn said. "Elizabeth is her name."

"Well, I hope she's not like Longshanks."

"Oh no, I don't think so. Nothing like him, I think." But Yrynn didn't really know for sure. "She wears hats—lots of hats—when she's not wearing her crown. We studied them in Helfenbunn's class, Two-legs Vigilance."

"But now there is really a problem." Lorna looked deeply concerned, and Yrynn found herself wondering. What could possibly be a problem once one had been murdered and dead for nearly a thousand years? Dead creatures weren't supposed to have any more problems.

"Yes? So, what's the problem?"

"During the earthquake, the real stone that had been brought to our village, the true stone, was lost, and we know we can't settle our bones until it is found." She gazed up at the wattling in the ceiling of Yrynn's lodge. "Everything is all askew, you know. Topsy-turvy."

"But how do you know this—that the bones won't settle until the real stone is found?"

Yrynn could have sworn that Lorna had taken a deep breath and sighed. But that was impossible. She was dead. Ghosts don't breathe.

Lorna appeared to shake her skull. The tufts of pale red hair quivered like small flames. "It's amazing you still have your lodge with everything all topsy-turvy. The stone gone and all that."

"Yes, but that's kind of a problem for me."

"How can it be a problem?" Lorna asked.

"They say that my lodge was the only one that wasn't damaged because I'm a maranth."

"Maranth?" Lorna asked.

"A witch."

"Oh no!" A terrified shadow crossed Lorna's luminous blue eyes.

"You know about maranths?"

Lorna leaned closer and peered into Yrynn's eyes. "They burned them!"

Yrynn leaned closer to the misty face. Like small blue bubbles, Lorna's eyes seemed to float eerily in the eye sockets of her skull. "Do you believe I'm a witch?"

"Of course not. My mother says only ignorant people believe in such things."

"People?"

"Two-legs. Humans."

"I see," Yrynn replied.

Lorna seemed to swell up again, as if she were taking a deep breath. Yrynn reminded herself that this was impossible. "I might be able to help you, Yrynn, and you can help me."

"Help you how?"

"Help me settle the bones. Help me and Fergus find the true stone. The Stone of Destiny. Once it's settled in its proper place, the bones will settle and we can return to Neamorra."

"Neamorra?"

"Heaven," Lorna replied softly.

"What is your heaven—Neamorra—like?"

"Belonging. That is what the word *Neamorra* really means. The Belong. Right now, Fergus and I are neither here nor there. We are in feasghair, the In-Between. That is the old word for where we are. But we need to belong."

There was another slight swirl of mist, as if a phantom breeze stirred through the wattling of the den.

"What is your heaven, Yrynn?"

"Oh, we call it the Great Pond. We think of it as being like those special days when the water is very, very still, during the time of the water lilies or the falling leaves. The pond is so black, it reflects the clouds. It's as if sky and water become one, and the reflections of the falling leaves or the lilies and the clouds are painted across the pond."

"Lovely," Lorna whispered, then paused. Suddenly her eyes seemed to grow brighter and sparkle with tears. "You need to help us, Yrynn. Help us."

Then something else stirred the air. Some bones embedded in a slow swirl of mist started to emerge.

A ghostly boy began to shimmer slightly. His bones were shrouded in the tattered bloodstained remnants of his tunic and breeches. His short and raggedy hair flared out from his head like a nimbus of pale fire.

"Come on, Fergus," his sister urged. "She's really nice. She's sort of like us."

"Like us?"

"She may not be dead, but she doesn't exactly belong."

Tears welled in the young beaver's eyes. "I know I don't belong, but I'm not a witch."

"Oh, I know that," Fergus said. He reached out and touched her fur.

She suddenly felt a sparkly warmth run through her. *Touched. Touched by a ghost!*

CHAPTER 16

Two-Legs Vigilance Class

"*A*nd so young kits, you recall in our lesson from last time that we discussed major characteristics of two-legs. How they move, how they walk. They can jump. They can even dance. But not as we do in the water during our courting or at our festival rituals." She narrowed her eyes and turned to look at Yrynn. As she locked the young beaver in her gaze, a bitter light glowed from her eyes. "Perhaps they dance like our young friend over there, Yrynn. Did you learn to log dance like your ancestors from Canada? Did they learn from the two-legs?"

"No ma'am. I've never seen such a creature in my life. Nor had my parents or grandparents or great-great-grandparents ever seen a two-legs." Yrynn, usually so docile, was now glaring at Castor Helfenbunn.

But I have! Dunwattle inwardly groaned. And why was Helfenbunn always picking on Yrynn? It wasn't her fault that her great-great-grandparents had come from Canada. Canuck Castors could sherd like no other beavers down the most boisterous rivers and streams, guiding the floating logs by skipping up and down them.

Yrynn felt a snarl coiling up inside her. *Where would these beavers be without Canucks like her and Buck and Fenno?* She knew where they'd be—half the lodges would not have been built in the pond. And there wouldn't be enough storage for winter food. Homeless and starving, that's where these snooty beavers would be!

"Now," continued Helfenbunn, "it is often said that two-legs can have an odor that is somewhat salty. This odor is especially strong when they sweat. We beavers do not sweat."

A young beaver raised a paw. "We have a lovely odor, don't we?"

"Yes, Percy. Our odor is produced by castoreum. A gut oil. And guess what?"

"What?" a few beavers asked in unison.

"Two-legs, humans, people love it. Yet another reason for them to kill us, aside from wanting our pelts to make coats and hats. They use our natural bodily fluids for perfume."

"Perfume?" another kit asked.

"Perfume is a scent created by humans from several ingredients to make them smell better." The young kits couldn't help but giggle. These two-legs seemed absolutely ridiculous to them, wearing hats and coats and then mixing up brews to make them smell better. A lot of silly work. Helfenbunn continued. "They love the smell of castoreum. They say it smells something like vanilla, which is used in one of their most popular foods, ice cream. I doubt we would like ice cream, as it tastes nothing like our delicious woods and barks."

Dunwattle was suddenly alert. Had he picked up the scent of the woman with the flashing hands? All he could remember was the flash. No smell. He had been too panicked to sniff.

Helfenbunn's class was held in a large lodge. She now pulled down a chart where two-legs had been drawn. "Our dear librarian, Kukla, has prepared these for you. Mistress Kukla, would you care to explain?"

A little fur ball of a beaver with flecks of gray in her pelt waddled forward.

"Hello, kits. It's lovely to be here today."

"Hello, Mistress Kukla," the kits replied in unison. They all loved the librarian. She always found a book that was just perfect for them, no matter who they were. She often served them snacks—special snacks like acorns dipped in sticky moss or liverwort tea or sweet scum balls that had been rolled in the syrup of leaking maple trees, one of the best treats ever.

"Now, kits," Mistress Kukla began. "The last time we met I believe I explained some of the basic differences between the two-legs and ourselves. Can anyone remember?"

Retta's paw shot up in the air. "They walk on their long legs."

Yrynn felt a shiver creep through her as she recalled what Lorna had told her about the murderous two-legs king, Edward Longshank, with his very long legs.

"And they don't have fur but hair." Retta began rattling off all sorts of facts about two-legs.

Meanwhile Dunwattle was cringing at the back of the lodge, vividly recalling his own encounter. It was as if that flash had finally receded and now left a clear image of the creature in his mind.

Mistress Kukla continued speaking. "Now, because two-legs have no fur, they wear what are called clothes. I have brought some pictures from a book, *Fashion through the Ages*." She propped open a rather large book that Elsinore must have scavenged for her. "This first picture that we see is what two-legs call skirts. Females of the species often wear them." In that moment a crisp memory flared in both Dunwattle's and Yrynn's heads. Yrynn saw the tattered cloth that hung from the ghost Lorna's waist. Dunwattle recalled his encounter with horror—her bright green skirt with pictures of birds, very pretty-looking birds with colorful wings. How perfectly odd! And strange that he had not remembered those birds until this moment. He raised his paw shyly.

"Yes, Dunwattle. Do you have a question?"

"Do the two-leg females always wear the same color skirt?"

"Oh no, not at all. Skirts are made of fabric, and the fabric comes in all sorts of colors. Often there are pictures and designs woven fabric like . . . shapes and flowers, maybe leaves and—"

"Birds?" Dunwattle almost whispered the word.

"Oh yes, birds certainly might be part of a pattern."

Locksley had settled next to Dunwattle and gave him a poke. The message was clear. *Shut up!*

"How very clever of you, Dunwattle. What an imagination you have."

Oh, Mistress Kukla, if you only knew! Dunwattle thought as dread crept through him.

Yrynn glanced in his direction. *Curious,* she thought. Lorna had mentioned how Dunwattle had fallen to pieces when she had appeared in his lodge, but she certainly wasn't wearing any skirt with birds. No one could have mistaken those bloodstains for birds.

Castor Helfenbunn stepped forward. "Thank you,

Mistress Kukla, for sharing your knowledge with us. Most enlightening. As you recall, kits, I explained in our previous lesson that female two-legs are usually smaller than males. They are shorter and do not weigh as much. Quite different from us, isn't it?"

"I'll say!" Percy exclaimed. "How come male two-legs get to be bigger and weigh more and we don't?"

"It's our brains," Clover barked. "We female beavers have got bigger brains."

"Yes . . . absolutely!" the girl beavers all shouted.

"Class! Class!" Castor Helfenbunn shouted as she rapped with her hickory stick on the wattled wall. "Order, please. Order."

Yrynn shyly raised her paw. "Yes, Yrynn? You have something to say?" Mistress Kukla asked.

"Why bother with her?" Retta muttered to Gorsa. "She's a you-know. . . ."

But Mistress Kukla overheard and immediately bristled up to what looked like twice her normal size. "Oh, but I do. Every kit needs to be listened to." She then turned to Yrynn. "You have something to say, Yrynn?"

"It's just a thought, Mistress Kukla."

"I'm interested in thoughts. Share your thought with us."

"Well, I was thinking maybe female beavers are large because you know . . . they have to get fat for when their babies are born. Because they have to give them milk. Lots of milk so they'll grow."

"Well, my goodness gracious!" Mistress Kukla exclaimed. "That is a wonderful thought and a very sensible one at that. Thank you, Yrynn, for sharing." She sent a darting glance toward Castor Helfenbunn. "What do you think, Castor Helfenbunn?"

But the Castor merely sniffed haughtily. "I think perhaps you are allowing too much freethinking in this classroom. The kits might not be ready for these kinds of facts of life."

"Well, facts of life might be helpful in avoiding facts of death," Mistress Kukla said dryly.

A silence had descended on the lodge. The kits were somewhat incredulous. They knew that an argument between grown-ups had almost broken out. It could have grown into a fierce fight. This rarely happened in the pond. They heard the splash as the librarian set her front paws into the underwater tunnel and slipped out of the school lodge. "And please come and visit the library anytime, kits," she called back.

Helfenbunn stiffened. "Class dismissed!" she announced. The kits rushed for tunnel. "No crowding in the water tunnel, please!" she called after them.

"I feel sorry for Yrynn. Don't you, Locksley?" Dunwattle asked.

"Well, yes, but honestly, Dunwattle, I've got more on

my mind at the moment than just Yrynn. When you saw the you-know-what, was it bigger or smaller than the other you-know-what that you saw?"

Dunwattle's voice dropped. "You mean was the living you-know-what bigger than the dead you-know-what? Uh ... the ghost? It's not really a fair comparison, for Castor's sake!"

"Don't curse, Dunwattle. All I did was ask you a question."

"I don't know the answer. One was a grown-up, and the other was a kit. I think they call them a child. And I still feel sorry for Yrynn. Everyone treats her like sludge."

They slipped out of the school lodge into the exit water tunnel. Swim left and they would slide into the Froglands, thick with lily pads. Go right, they would be in Mistress Kukla's library. Dunwattle caught a glimpse of Yrynn's tail headed just that way.

Where's Dunwattle going now? Locksley wondered, but followed him anyway.

"Oh yes, dear," they heard Mistress Kukla saying to Yrynn. "It's a challenging task to dress like a human. Since they don't have fur, they need to keep warm. Not to mention the fact that their skin is not really waterproof. So they wear different kinds of clothes for different seasons. In winter they wear many layers of clothing, but in summer they dress lighter. I have a book here. Somewhat ancient. Many of these garments might have gone out of style, but take a look at this book, Yrynn." Mistress Kukla took down a large book from an upper shelf and opened it up. "Oh, hello there, young'uns, you interested too?"

The three young beavers pored over a grand picture of a very grand lady. "Lady" was the word Helfenbunn used when speaking of female beavers.

"Goodness!" Yrynn exclaimed. "So fancy."

"Well, yes indeed, she is a queen. That's her crown. The dress is white satin embroidered with all sorts of pictures of things she liked, I suppose. There is of course a rose—the Tudor Rose, I believe they call it. And there's a silver fern."

Yrynn suddenly became very excited. "Look at that!" she exclaimed, pointing with a claw of her paw.

"What is it?" Locksley asked.

"It's the Canadian maple leaf—a Canuck leaf. How about that?"

Dunwattle looked at Yrynn. "You should tell Helfenbunn. Tell her a queen wears a Canuck leaf."

However, thought Yrynn, *perhaps she's not really a queen, because the Coronation Stone that sits beneath the throne is not the true stone. So perhaps she is not a true queen.* But Yrynn said none of this.

"Yes, yes," Kukla said. "Perhaps I should tell Helfenbunn." The librarian found herself in an uncomfortable situation. She knew that Helfenbunn had objected to some of the books she had in the library and had suggested removing them. But Kukla had threatened to go to the Castorium. She was in a difficult situation. She patted the costume book gently with her paw. She had an obligation to these kits and an obligation to the books. She did not want to endanger either the books or the kits. She certainly agreed with Dunwattle that Helfenbunn treated Canuck Castors unfairly. But she was uncertain about what she could do about it. The words she had said to Helfenbunn just a few minutes before were among the harshest she had ever uttered. She didn't like the feeling. She did not want to pick a fight with those who wielded more power than she did in the hierarchy of the pond. Kukla had only recently been elected to the Castorium. It was significant as it was the first time a pond librarian had ever been elected to that distinguished body. It seemed odd to Kukla that it had taken so long for her to be elected, as she was probably the most well-read concerning the history of the pond.

Dunwattle began to speak. "Do you have any pictures of young two-legs . . . er . . . not dressed in these fancy gowns as you call them but in shorter, kind of tattered . . . cloth?"

Yrynn felt her heart plunge to her gut. Her skeat seemed to shriek at Dunwattle's question. *Yes, bloodstained, tattered clothes* . . . A terrible queasiness flooded her. So Dunwattle had seen Lorna too. It unnerved her. She dared not look at him. Then at just that moment there was the long warbling hoot of a boreal owl from the spruce tree that grew at the edge of the pond.

"Ah, the boreal sounds!" Kukla said brightly. "Time for the creed."

Saved by the owl! Yrynn thought.

And as the three beavers swam out of the rear water exit from the library, they saw the first patch of stars lifting into the darkening sky. On this windless night, the water had a purple sheen from the remnant light of the setting sun. The black silhouettes of dozens of beavers perched atop the more than two dozen domed roofs of their lodges began to chant the "Creed of the Castors of the Pond of Glendunny."

I am a Castor of Glendunny.
I seek nothing but what is my right to have.
I am a guardian of the earth,
A species meant to create water, conserve water,
To tend ponds so other creatures may flourish.
Therefore, if there is a tree, we cut it.
If there is a stream, we block it.
Running water must be halted.
In destruction is our preservation.
Great Castor's will is our way.

CHAPTER 17

"Just a Canuck"

"All right, listen up." Brora, an immense beaver, stood atop the lodge of First Guild, where the Castorium generally met. "Chomp Three, where be you?" Brora bellowed.

"Over here, dear." Brora's mate, Eldon, a spindly little fellow, waved. He so admired his mate, Brora, who had become chief of Chomp Three, one that specialized in detecting the smallest of dam leaks. He gave her his special wink, short for, "Hey there, Buttercup!" It was in a thicket of buttercups that grew at the edge of the pond where they had had their first courting dance and then slipped into the water to continue it. There was nothing like dancing in the water on a night streaked with moonlight, folding one's arms around a beloved.

"All right, Eldon. Though we're almost to the summer solstice, it's nearly too late to begin stockpiling for winter. I'm worried about the store lodge on the bank. The banks have eroded. We've got to keep that stored wood dry. During a pond swell in the rainy season, our supplies could be damaged. So I'm going to take a few from Chomp Three to check for leaks in the store lodge."

She turned her head and began to address a small cluster of beavers. "Now, the willows in East Marsh are ready for cutting, and we'll have to drag them in for winter storage. I'll need some draggers."

Yrynn shuddered. Canucks usually made up drag units. Very boring unless there was guiding or sherding large logs on lively rivers or streams. But dragging willows across land was monotonous.

"Chomp Two." Brora swiveled her head.

"Here, madam," called a beaver named Red Tip. The tips of his fur matched the red mud the Castors hauled for wattling. Red Tip was an expert in lacing the slender limbs and branches into what was called a "complication," a kind of latticework screen that was plastered with mud.

"Ah, Red Tip. The good news is there are some scrumptious aspens ready for cutting over near the eagle's nest. The not-so-good news is that they're growing at the base of the cedar forest. We all know the rules about the cedar forest. No trespassing."

Of course, Brora wouldn't say anything to indicate why this was a forbidden zone, nor would anyone else. And yet they all knew—it was the Rar Wolves that were rumored to haunt this forest. No beaver had ever seen one, yet the stories of them lingered. They were the great unnamed menace. *Blaiddiad Rar* was the whole name for the unnamed creature. The word *Blaiddiad* actually meant, "One Who Cannot Be Named" in the old Castor language, and *Rar* was the word for "wolves." By not naming these creatures, this menace became even more terrifying.

The Rar Wolves were said to linger in the forest of the cedars. These trees were known for their exceptionally long lives. Some lived well over a thousand years. The beavers found the trees' longevity eerie and intimidating. They said old spirits lived in these trees that saw everything. So the Castors of Glendunny came to think of the trees as the Eyes of the Woods. Some believed the indestructible cedars possessed mysterious powers. Along with the wolves who could not be named, the cedar forest had become a kind of hell on earth. Something to be feared and dreaded. Awesome and vile.

Brora sensed the anxiety that shivered through the young kits. "The stories of the cedar forest need not frighten us as long as we respect the woods. Is that understood?" she asked.

There was a wave of murmured voices that spread across

the pond. "Yes, Castor Brora."

Brora then announced the remaining details for wattling and wood gathering and which of the eight dams and various lodges would be needing work.

"Now, Chomp captains, pick the young'uns you want on your Chomp and get to work.

"Oh, I just hope I don't get put on my mum and da's Chomp," Dunwattle whispered.

"And I don't want to be on my parents' Chomp either," Locksley said. "It's so boring when you have to work with your parents. They always want to make sure they don't treat you better or favor you. Then you end up getting the worst jobs."

Yrynn looked at them. She could not help but think what she would give to be with her own parents on a Chomp. Would she ever stop missing them? It had been almost a year since they had disappeared. "Missing and presumed dead"—that was the term that the beavers used. "Presumed." The word haunted her. Presumed dead was not dead-dead. Maybe it was more like a ghost, a haint? Would it frighten her to meet up with her mum's or da's ghost? She was used to ghosts, after all. She'd gotten used to Lorna and Fergus. But then again, maybe only two-legs—or humans— could become ghosts. She'd never heard of a ghost beaver.

"All right," Red Tip called out. "I want—let's see— Simon and Retta, Dunwattle, Locksley, and yes, we'll need a dragger. So how about the Canuck Yrynn—you come along."

"I just don't think it's right," Locksley hissed, in what he thought was a whisper. "They always single her out as being a Canuck. She's much more. And besides, my mum told me we learned a lot from those Canadian beavers."

"Don't be silly," said Retta.

"Silly about what?"

"The Canucks. They're quite inferior."

"Inferior to what?" Dunwattle spun around.

"To us."

"And what's so great about us?" Dunwattle asked.

"Dunwattle, how can you say such a thing? Your grandmother, Wanda the Wattler, and Locksley's parents, descended from Avalinda. Your heritage, both of yours, is extremely distinguished," Retta said.

Locksley felt the *grrrr* begin to stir within him. The grrrr was a sound, a blend of anger and complete contempt, that was common to beavers who were experiencing deeply negative feelings. It gurgled up within them and was a noise halfway between a very deep growl and a bark. He tried to quell it. He and Dunwattle were going to have to work with Retta, chewing through aspens, and then on the complication with Red Tip for the store lodge at the edge of the pond. There were bound to be many more grrrs stirring in his gut.

"Don't flip a tail, Locksley. She's just a dragger. That's all she can do," Retta said. "Look, Locksley. Yrynn is what she is."

Dunwattle was now seething. Through his clenched orange front teeth, he growled. "And you, Retta, are what you are. A vile little skimpcrizzle. Yes, your skimp reeks of crizzle!"

This was one of the worst insults a beaver could hurl at another. Crizzle was a noxious odor that emanated from meat eaters such as lynx and wolves and bears. Quite the opposite of beaver odors and the vanilla scent that two-legs sought for their perfumes and ice cream.

Retta began to tremble. Her eyes welled up. "I'm going to tell on you. I'm going straight to Red Tip and tell him exactly what you said. No! I might even go to Brora. She'll be furious!"

"Oh, go suck a pile of stinkweed," Dunwattle replied calmly.

But Brora couldn't have cared less. "I'm not here to referee squabbles, Retta. Don't get your tail in a twist. Get that beaver butt of yours back to Chomp Two with Red Tip and don't bother him with your nonsense." Brora thwacked her tail hard on the ground, making a loud noise. The other beavers stopped what they were doing. It did not bode well to irritate the chief of Chomp Three. Retta appeared to shrink. She turned her head toward them, and Dunwattle and Locksley both caught the glare in her dark eyes. It seemed to cut right into them. Retta was mean and nasty, like her great-aunt Tonk. And it did not pay to cross Tonk.

CHAPTER 18

A Complication in More Ways than One

Chomp Three had very swiftly gnawed their way through a great quantity of sticks. And now Brunwella, a seasoned wattler, had arrived to demonstrate the best pattern for the complication, the latticework screen.

Brunwella surveyed the pile of slender limbs. Scratching her head, she turned to Red Tip. "So, what do you think?"

"Well, it all depends on the type of mud. You've got low-silt mud around here. So I think you have to drive the verticals in deeper. That means number-four-size verticals, then you have to weave through the most slender horizontal aspen branches, say number-two size, alternating with number-threes. It's your basic Wanda pattern, bless her heart. She used it so often in low-silt situations like this.

Now all this should be set on some biggies. Are there some upstream? Danceables?" Red Tip asked.

"Indeed. You got a Canuck in your group?" Brunwella stood up on her hind legs and surveyed the kits.

Dunwattle clamped his eyes shut and winced. He'd heard this word *Canuck* a thousand times, but why did it seem to grate now in his small rounded ears? He closed the inner flaps instantly. Something just didn't seem right about calling these New World beavers such a name. But Dunwattle realized that he had probably used that word countless times without ever thinking it was wrong. Why now? Was it just because he felt sorry for Yrynn, for the ruthless teasing she endured? She was an orphan. So alone. Beaver kits often got teased. They had squabbles with friends or were scolded by a teacher. But they could always turn to their parents for some sort of comfort. Who could Yrynn turn to?

"We do have a Canuck. Yrynn, come over here, lassie," Red Tip called. Yrynn made her way over. "Brunwella has a big log, just what we need, upstream from here. Can you dance it down?"

"Yes . . . yes . . . happy do to it."

"You'll need a pusher too, won't you?"

"It helps," she replied. Red Tip looked around. "Think we've run out of Canucks here."

"I'll do it!" Dunwattle lifted a front paw.

"He ain't a Canuck, is he?" someone said, and there was a smattering of laughter.

"Shut your trap, Levi," Red Tip barked.

"Yes sir." Levi was a large kit, but he appeared to shrink back into his pelt, which suddenly seemed too big for him.

"Thank you for your offer, Dunwattle. You go upstream with Yrynn here. I'm sure she can teach you the tricks for this river."

"Yes sir."

"I can go too!" Locksley volunteered.

"No," Red Tip replied. "You stay here and work on getting stones and mud for the wattling."

"You're much too good for that kind of work on the river," Retta whispered, and tipped her head flirtatiously toward Locksley.

"What are you talking about?" Fire seemed to spike from Locksley's dark eyes. This was not the response that Retta had hoped for, and he didn't give her time to answer. "What they do is amazing."

"The Canucks? Are you kidding me?"

"No, I'm not kidding. And I think it's high time we stop calling them Canucks. It seems wrong. Not nice. Not nice at all."

"Not nice? They aren't nice. They're crude, stupid creatures."

"They are Castors!" Locksley replied. The three words

were not loud but scalding. "This pond of Glendunny would have dried up centuries ago if the Canucks hadn't arrived." He turned his back and trundled off to find some good stones.

The river reflecting the light of the moon ran like a sparkling ribbon through the night. Shadow figures gamboled against the surface of the water. It was a watery spectacle on the glazed silver of the river, with the silhouettes of trees, the wing prints of night birds, and the shadow of one dancing beaver. Stepping lively, Yrynn guided the rolling log through the currents and shoals of the rushing river. And then lacing the night were the twinkling conversations of thousands of fireflies. :—:*—-. Yrynn looked up at the fireflies and translated the flashes. *Dunwattle is good at this!* "Right you are," she whispered back. A firefly flashed again. +== . . . : *And he's not even a Canuck*, Yrynn translated. They whispered back, "He's excellent!" Yrynn was fluent in the firefly language.

And Dunwattle was good, very good, Yrynn thought as he pushed steadily from behind on the log as she rolled it. That's what it took to move a log smoothly through a boisterous watercourse, pushing and fine-tuned rolling. Together they could guide the log safely. Yrynn muffled a snort. These Old World beavers were a funny lot. OWBs was what they were often called. The OWBs were always looking down their snouts at the New World Canadian beavers. NWBs, as the OWBs said. Yet Yrynn knew that most times they just settled on "Canucks." An ugly-sounding word. If one named something with an ugly sound, it was almost like that creature became ugly in everyone's mind. To name something was very powerful. It was as if it gave one authority over a creature. Names had power, Yrynn thought.

She often wondered if it was the difference of their pelts that had marked them, singled them out for their particular destiny. It was so easy to be contemptuous of something that was not exactly like you—a different color, a different way of speaking or swimming or gnawing a log. Dunwattle would have never been a pusher for her if Skipper had been available. *But Great Castor!* Yrynn thought, Dunwattle seemed to be a natural. Who knew, maybe he had some Canuck blood after all. Yes, he was a descendant of Avalinda, the Aquarius of Great Fosters, but perhaps she had fallen in love with a lowly Canuck! Never could tell. When romance struck, what was to stop them? Yrynn had heard tales about Canucks and Old World beavers running off into the woods together, then returning a few moons later when three or four, sometimes even six kits popped out. Surprise!

Such thoughts were passing through Yrynn's mind. It would be nice, she thought, if she could have a real friend.

Not just a ghost of a two-legs for a friend. *No offense, Lorna,* she thought. But she was sure that Lorna would understand. She could now hear little puffs coming from the stern end of the log. Dunwattle pushed and cajoled the log out of rowdy shallows, with their capricious currents, into the deeper and calmer water. In the next stretch of calm, she would dance back and talk to him a bit. She could talk and roll a log at the same time. She was that good. Some old Canucks said she was fabulous! What a lovely word, *fabulous!* She could almost taste it—like mint moss!

In Dunwattle's eyes she was more than fabulous. She was fantastic, stupendous, exquisite—stellar! Yes, stellar, as bright as any star in the Castor constellation—a sparkling winter constellation. He nosed the log, a true biggie, to the other side of the river to avoid a patch of swirling eddies. She could probably ride right through it. He could hardly take his eyes off her beautiful dancing feet as she tiptoed up and down the log, rolling it this way and that, avoiding every buried river snag or lurking water devil. A water devil was an unpredictable whirlpool that could pop up from the depths of a river and actually flip a log end over end.

Yrynn's pelt was lustrous in the moonlight. A tawny hue with hints of bright gold. It was as if a secret sun glowed deep within her fur. Canucks tended toward the paler colors of the fur spectrum. And all the while, Dunwattle diligently guided the log as he basked in the golden glow of Yrynn's pelt. But it wasn't simply her pelt. Those eyes, those adorable ears, he thought as she daintily picked her way from one end of the log to the other. He began to compose a poem in his head.

How do I love thee?
Let me count the ways....
The moonlight on your pelt
On a summer's night
Or would it be the sparkling frost
When winter's woe is upon us
and all is frozen
But my love for thee....

Dunwattle stopped. What would come next? There were so many words that could rhyme with thee—*me, tea, pee....* Oh no no! Possibly tree. But Yrynn wasn't like a tree at all. She was round and soft.

A river otter drifted by as he was midway through composing his love poem. She had two pups balanced on her belly. Tiny little things, not more than a few days old. Dunwattle glanced at them. They were very sweet looking, all cuddled up on their mum's tummy as she floated on her back down the river in the moonlight. *Was there anything cozier?* Dunwattle wondered. He'd been told that the otters of Glendunny were slightly different from most river otters, as they often swam on their backs like sea otters cradling their infants. It was thought that they might have come from that New World across the sea, like the Canucks, and had perhaps lived with the sea otters and bred with them. Hence, they had learned this way of transporting their young. So cozy!

Dunwattle loved his own mum; all beavers did. But beaver parents weren't really snuggly or playful. It was always about work and training to be the best Chomp member possible. The best wattler, the best diver for good mud, the best gnawer or bark stripper. It was always work work work for beaver kits! And since they swam almost from the minute they were born, unlike otters, there wasn't a chance for surfing down a river on their mum's belly. And here this otter was crooning a little tune to her pups. The song was saying something about Lontra. Dunwattle had learned from Castor Feltch that Lontra was the river otters' creator, the way the Great Castor was the beavers' creator.

The otter with her pups was now sculling over to take a closer look at the log Dunwattle was pushing.

"Hello," the otter greeted Dunwattle, and inhaled a deep breath. "A lovely night for a swim."

"Indeed, ma'am. Hello, pups," Dunwattle greeted them. "So, you're out for a moonlight romp with mum, are you?" The pups made a few little squeaking noises in response.

"Now be sure to make a star wish," Dunwattle said cheerfully. "The Swan is rising. See the star in its tail? That's Deneb. Very good for star wishes." He had learned about Deneb from Elsinore. It seemed to Dunwattle that he and Locksley learned more from the swan than they ever had from any Castor.

The otter took another deep sniff as she came closer to Dunwattle and then began to swim away with her pups before he could ask her name.

CHAPTER 19

The Otter's Lament

"*Oh, pups.*" *Glory sighed as she sculled back upstream to her den* carved out of the riverbank. "He is the one," she moaned. "Dunwattle." She recognized him as the son of Berta and Grizzmore and grandson of the famed Wanda the Wattler. She knew the scent of him, the family scent, and not only that but the scent of the waters from afar where he had been swimming. She began to untangle the web of scents that had filtered through her mind as she approached Dunwattle. One of those scents was that of a distant river far to the south. What had a young kit been doing down there in the lower Tweed? He had the pungent scent of that salmon river all over him. Luckily his parents didn't have the keen sense of smell that an otter had, or they'd be furious. What should she do? The poisonous words of the lynx Grinfyll still blistered in her ears.

That poor family. They had lost the wonderful Wanda, and surely this other kit would be either cast out of the pond or, worse, murdered by Grinfyll. But what choice did she have? If she didn't tell the lynx, her own pups would be murdered. And it would hardly take a curse of lynx to do in Iggy and Edy. One bite and they would be swallowed whole! Both of them. But what would happen if she didn't tell? If she and the pups just vanished?

She thought about all of this as she swam back to her own den in the riverbank. Climbing out, she held the two pups close to her chest. They nestled deep into her fur. She could feel their tiny hearts beating with hers. She looked up at the sky and felt a shudder pass through her. Hours ago, the stars Iglemore and Edlmyn had slipped west into another day on the far side of the previous night. If only she and her pups could follow them—go west with the stars. But soon she would be seeing the paws of Felis, the lynx constellation. What a terrible omen this was. Not even the stars were on her side! Dim and misty, the dreadful constellation started to rise. The starry lynx began to claw its way across the coming night. By morning all the stars would have dissolved. If only she could swim away into another world with her precious pups. Or might she go west?

She could at least try. She had to try. There was no other

choice. She listened to the sounds of the night, every sound, and every tiny critter seemed to chant, *Go . . . go . . . go, Glory, with your pups.* Nevertheless, she felt that first she had to confirm that it was indeed Dunwattle who bore the scent. And if he did, was there any way she could warn him? She would need to visit the pond. Mornings were best to go to the pond, for that was when the beavers returned from their night's work on the river and dams to their lodges to rest. Although even then they seemed to find numerous tasks to do. These creatures rarely rested, she mused to herself, as she watched an entire family and their kits repairing the roof of their lodge. Their energy was amazing. If they weren't chopping down trees in the forest, they were diving for mud and stones in the pond for wattling. There were perhaps thirty or more lodges in the big pond. All the beavers were very friendly and seemed to welcome otter visits. She knew many of them. They would make a big fuss over the cute otter babies and had endless questions about when they would begin to swim on their own. How were they taught to swim? How long did they nurse? Was it true they ate snails? If their teeth were strong enough to eat snails, why did they never try chewing bark, cutting trees? Much tastier than a snail.

So the next morning, Glory arrived at the pond and began a slow paddle in and around the many lodges. Some of the beavers she knew. Kukla, the librarian, was quite fond of her, as was Castor Feltch. She swam and she sniffed very carefully—otters had a way of deciphering each scent that emanated from a lodge. She would then tuck it away in her *cof,* a particular part of the otter brain that decoded scents. The family scents were the easiest to crack.

As she was approaching Dunwattle's lodge, she closed her eyes and sniffed. The scent of the River Tweed was overpowering. *Oh dear!* she thought. *This kit is doomed. And if not, then my own pups are doomed instead.*

CHAPTER 20

Dunwattle
in Love

Mist and sun, she glows,
Then dissolves into the trees.
My heart breaks, oh Yrynn!

He *scribbled on a piece of birch bark with the stiff reed of a pond willow.*

Why, Dunwattle asked himself for the one thousandth time, had Yrynn gone off? Just run off like that after she had ridden the big log back to the store lodge? He had so much he wanted to say to her. But after they had delivered the log to Chomp Three, she just barked out, "Thanks," and left. She had headed in the direction of the ancient cedar forest, the Eyes of the Forest. She seemed almost anxious to get there. Anxious but not nervous at all. Was she not worried about the Rar Wolves? Those spirits that were said to lurk in the very bark of the trees? Apparently not, for she waddled off with a determined gait—almost as if she were skipping! And was she even humming a little tune of some sort?

Truth be told, Yrynn, like many Canucks—or more properly New World beavers—had no fear of Rar Wolves, or any wolves, for that matter. They had grown up with them in Canada. The wolves were part of their history and their legends.

There was a time when the snow began to fall thickly in Canada that the wolf constellation and the Castor constellation frolicked side by side in the autumn sky for a few brief nights. It was the only time of the year they did so. Here in the Old World those stars and their constellations were not as visible. And they never appeared in winter but toward the end of summer. The beavers of Glendunny hardly noticed them. There were two small stars that burned bright blue. One belonged to the Castor constellation, and the other little one that tagged along was a wandering star from the wolf constellation, called Little Blue by the Castors of Canada. The stars of the wolf pup and the beaver kit were only dimly visible for a few hours during these summer nights in the Old World. But in the New World, every Canadian beaver told the stories—the Spirit Legends, of the adventures of Little Blue, the wolf star, and his best friend,

Little Beaver— to their young'uns.

So for Yrynn, the cedar woods held no fear, especially since she had heard countless stories in the brief time she had shared with her mum and da. In their cozy lodge, she had heard of the wolves and the beavers and how the Little Blue wolf star tagged after the beaver kit across the snowy nights in the great woods of Canada. The same stories that Yrynn had tried to tell to Lorna. Her own parents had told her these stories the first time they had taken her into the cedar woods. They said it was the proper place for her to hear these star stories of the New World. It was so exciting that first time they had taken her here as a tiny kit. She was sure the Old World beavers of the pond would have frowned upon such an adventure.

But when the stories began to grow dim in Yrynn's mind, she had decided to return to these forbidden woods. She felt safe in this place. Little by little, the stories started to come back to her, seep into her memory. At first, they were like the trickle of a slow-moving stream, but more recently they had become a true percolation of lively, bubbling water. Sooner or later she felt that Little Blue's true name would come to her. And then the story would be complete. But her mum had told her that stories were never really complete. They could always go on.

Dunwattle could not imagine why Yrynn would go off into those dreadful woods. This was breaking the rules and breaking his heart as he watched her dissolve into that menacing forest. She had hardly thanked him. Dunwattle thought he had done an excellent guiding job. A fog had rolled in thick, as it sometimes did toward dawn. No one would have seen her. But he had followed as long as he could, keeping the burnished glow of her pelt in sight until the moon slipped away.

In the dawn mists, Dunwattle had swum with the others back to the pond. Most likely no one would miss her. That was the way it went with Canucks. They were in a sense invisible to the rest of the world. When Yrynn's own parents had vanished, no one really seemed to care that much. There were perhaps scattered comments. "Well, they were getting old. . . ." "How long could they keep up that log dancing? Others can do it now." "Young 'nucks coming up . . ." "Those Canucks multiply like mosquitoes in stagnant water."

At the time, when Dunwattle had heard this crude remark about the mosquitoes, he hadn't thought much about it. But now he was furious. How outrageous it was to compare a Castor, a bright, industrious, sensitive mammal, a member of the rodent family, to an annoying, toothless little insect. A spineless little insect that laid its eggs in stinky water. It was disgraceful. How dare they compare Yrynn's parents, those fur-clad vertebrates, to those pesky, spineless bugs? With a single slap of a beaver tail, you could wipe out a dozen at once. Grown-ups could really be mean—mean and nasty.

Although guiding the log had been fairly exhausting, that morning Dunwattle couldn't sleep. So he had written two more poems. In between he kept popping up to peer out to see if he could spy Yrynn swimming back to Lower Scum, where she lived all by herself in the lodge of her vanished parents.

"Honestly, Dunwattle," his mother, Berta, called up from her sleeping chamber. "Why are you so restless? You've been sloshing about in and out of the back tunnel to the pond a dozen times at least."

"Er . . . uh . . . I just went out to dive for a rounder. I think I need it to patch my feeding shelf. The birch shreds are getting damp."

"Well, dear, if you really want to improve this lodge, your da and I are considering expanding the mudroom into a kind of play space. And you could help." Berta, Dunwattle's mum, was what his da called a serial renovator. She was always figuring out new improvements for their lodge.

"Why? We don't need a play space," Dunwattle whined.

"Well, dearie, guess what?"

Oh no . . . ! Dunwattle thought.

"Yes! I can see from the look on your face, you're as excited as I am."

Not! "But Mum. Alfred and Josie just moved out last summer and . . ."

"I know you miss your big brother and sister, and you need some playmates, dearie."

"Mum, I'm almost grown. I don't need babies around."

"Yes you do."

"Mum, I don't want to play. I want to work. And I already have a friend to 'play' with—Locksley is my very best friend." He wouldn't dare mention Yrynn. What would his mum do if she thought he had feelings, deep feelings for a Canuck? His family came from a long line of the most distinguished pond Castors of Great Fosters. And of course his grandmother Wanda the Wattler was renowned. There had been a full moon cycle of mourning after she died, when the curse of lynx had torn her to shreds.

"Well, you can work by helping me with the young'uns."

Dunwattle was simply speechless. *Oh yeah, just what I want to do! Any more great ideas, Mum?*

"Come on, dear. It will be fun. It's been so long since your da and I have had little itty-bitty kitties frolicking about. You're almost all grown up now." *Exactly*, Dunwattle thought, and frolicking with itty-bitties was not his idea of fun.

"Mum, I am almost grown up."

"I know. And I know it can be a difficult age."

"No, Mum, old age is supposed to be difficult. Not my age. Remember Grandma Wanda's lower back problems and then the stiffness in her tail? She could hardly give a good water slap with it. My age is supposed to be fun! Or at least a little bit of fun, when I'm not working all the time."

"First of all, Wanda never let age interfere with her wattling, nor her leadership. Now, I know you did a wonderful job pushing the log that the Canuck was dancing down the river."

"Her name is Yrynn, Mum. She has a name. Don't call her a Canuck."

"Oh dear," Berta mumbled. The two words barely squeezed out through her inner lips. All beavers had inner lips behind their front teeth to keep the water out when they carried sticks while swimming. And it seemed as if she was trying very hard not to say all she wanted to and let too much water in!

"Don't speak behind your lips, Mum. I know what you're thinking. You don't think I should know a Canuck or have one as a friend."

"I didn't say that," Berta replied.

"No, you didn't say it out loud. You just moaned when I asked you to call her Yrynn and not a Canuck."

His mum winced. "I see no need to continue this

conversation, Dunwattle."

"I don't either," he snapped.

"Tone, Dunwattle. Tone! Don't speak rudely to your mother." His father, Grizzmore, had just arrived home.

"I'm going to sleep." Dunwattle pouted and lumbered up another tunnel to his sleeping chamber. He was just about to settle into the freshly shredded aspen of his bed when he gasped. He saw there was something taking shape! A mist hovered, and out of the mist a shape emerged that was furless but with two legs. It began to assemble itself on the pillow of moss where he would lay his head. His eyes opened wide. The bones were back! Back and even more frightening. Melting out of a mist were the tattered shreds, not of bark but cloth—clothing! Clothing like Kukla had shown them. But these clothes were not the gown of a queen. Not like Queen Elizabeth's made of white satin with all sorts of little designs on it. Nor were they like the green skirt with the bird pictures on it, like worn by the two-legs on the riverbank. No, this "gown" was stained with blood.

"Oh, Great Castor!" he muttered now behind his two inner lips.

"Don't run away! Please!!!! I need you!" Lorna cried out. "Yrynn might help me."

"Yrynn?" Dunwattle gasped, and then fell into a swoon.

At this same hour of the morning, Yrynn made her way deeper and deeper into the Eyes of the Forest. The gigantic cedars cast a latticework of silent shadows as she walked. Her waddling gait left no trace. Land travel was never easy for a beaver, nothing like swimming, but now Yrynn felt as if she were perhaps dancing on a log down a very still river. Everything was soft and fluid. The paths carpeted with moss absorbed the sounds of her footsteps just as they had when she first entered this forest with her parents. Everything seemed untouched, untrodden, as if no creature had passed this way. And yet the ancient trees seemed to watch. They had knotholes that peered out through the dappled light. The trees were immense and unimaginably old. Yrynn had remembered her mum saying that they were in fact thousands upon thousands of years old. Their trunks were tall and craggy. Some had huge swelling bumps. As she went, she felt almost like she was trying to read the cloud pictures that spread across the sky on sunny days. Sometimes the cumulous white masses built into immense confections that resembled the castles of the two-legs that Kukla, the librarian, had told them about, or perhaps a gigantic wolf padding across the blue sky, or the slinking prowl of a lynx.

But there were no lynx in this forest nor wolves. No predators of any sort in these woods, Yrynn was sure. To her the forest felt . . . felt . . . She searched for a word.

Kindly. If anything, the gnarled trunks with their bulges and bumps reminded her of faces she had once upon a time known or perhaps had dreamed about. They could have belonged to any creature, either animal or two-legs. She did not give a thought to the Rar Wolves that were rumored to haunt this forest. The *Blaiddiad Rar,* as the beavers called them. This forest held a world and it was watching her. She was not anxious but peaceful. Serene. It was a timeless place.

She was uncertain how long she had been walking through the ancient trees. Why were the Castors so frightened of this forest? she wondered. For Yrynn it seemed as if the farther she walked, the more she felt that she was in a place that might be considered *heligh*—sacred. Her mother once tried to explain what the word meant. Perhaps she had been too young when her mum told her that heligh meant, "All that you hold most dear. The things that are buried deep in your *ama,* your soul." So, was this the land of souls? Then Yrynn recalled the ghost Lorna's words when she had asked her about the place that two-legs called heaven.

Belonging. She had said. *That is what the word* Neamorra *really means. The Belong.* Now Yrynn knew she was not dead, and she was not in that in-between place either. But this must be a kind of Belong, for she felt souls, the paws of her mum, her da pressing gently against her. And that feeling was sacred. Who needed heaven when they could be alive in these woods? This for Yrynn was the Belong! And the pond, she suddenly realized, had been a kind of feasghair on earth for her.

There was a low rumble of thunder to the north. She should get back to the lodge. She knew that Lorna would be waiting. She could not let her down. If there was a way to help Lorna and Fergus get to their Belong, she must. Fragments of their conversation came back to her.

I might be able to help you, Yrynn, and you can help me. . . .
Help me settle the bones. Help me and Fergus find the true
stone. The Stone of Destiny. Once it's settled in its proper
place, the bones will settle and we can return to Neamorra . . .
heaven. The Belong.

CHAPTER 21

Glory
in Despair

Glory tipped her head toward the darkening sky. Stacks of angry clouds were piling up. She had delayed for two days in telling Grinfyll what she had discovered. He had been back almost every day. These clouds seemed now to be a sign. The night would be foggy and starless, but she could keep those two stars in her mind's eye. They even seemed to beckon her. *Go! Go west and beat the night into another day! Go! Escape!* The sharp scent of the lower Tweed still lingered in her nostrils. She could swim there and then go on . . . and on . . . forever, perhaps. Even back to where her great-great-great-grandparents came from—across the sea to the New World and Canada! She knew it was important for the beavers of Glendunny to keep their existence secret. But no such rules bound otters to this place. *Canada, here we come!* Glory thought as she slid with her pups from her den in the riverbank.

"Come on now. Edy and Iggy, we can do this." She slipped into the water.

"But Mum, the river is rough. The water will splash us in our faces," Iggy said.

"I'm going in!" Edy said.

"In Iggy!" Glory snapped. "Remember what I have told you these last few days when we've practiced swimming. You have to lift your head out of the water! Great Lontra blessed you with a long neck to lift your head over this little chop."

"Little chop," Iggy muttered, and then coughed.

"See! Darling, you must keep your head high and your mouth shut! Like your sister, Edy."

Edy gave a slight smirk. Iggy lashed out at her.

"That's enough," hissed Glory. The pups immediately obeyed and quickly swam into the slipstream behind her that boosted their speed. Glory looked back. They were doing a good job, keeping close in her wake and rarely taking a mouthful of water.

After the better part of an hour, she turned to them. "Good work, pups. We can take a bit of a rest. Over to the bank now!"

"About time!" Iggy murmured. "Don't we have another den around here?"

"Yes, but that's not where we're going. We're going to a muskrat's den that I know."

There was an edge in Glory's voice that they had never heard before. They looked into the fierce light that emanated from her eyes. Overhead the entire sky flinched as lightning scalded the night and clawed at the sliver of the new moon. She looked at the pups. They were trembling with fear. Not fear of lightning, fear of their mother. She knew that to them she appeared transformed into something else—a stern, almost unknowable creature. But if this is what it took—well, there was no going back. No going back, literally. Only forward.

"Pups"—the light in her eyes softened just a bit—"we are swimming for our lives." She paused, took a deep breath. "There is something bad out there. Something that wants to kill us. Tear our throats out. Our eyes. Our hearts. We can never go back to our den."

"Not to any of our dens?" Edy asked.

"No, not the winter den nor the spring or the summer den."

"But we haven't even lived long enough to see the autumn den or the winter one," Edy said.

"Exactly, and if we stay here, you will never ever see them."

"But why, Mum? Why can't we go back? Where will we go?" Iggy asked.

"Away, far far away." She paused for a long time.

Iggy whispered, "Across . . . ?" His voice now trembled. "The Across?"

Glory nodded slowly. "Yes, pups, we're going to the Across."

The Across—no bays, no coves, no inlets or lakes or ponds. Just one immense river that two-legs and the other otters called the Sea. It was for the sea that these other otters were named sea otters. Most river otters simply called them "the Others."

"And . . . will those—the Others—welcome us?" Edy asked.

"First, dear Edy, we just have to survive. We have to get there. But I think the other otters should welcome us, as our histories are much entwined."

"Entwined?" Iggy asked.

"Woven together, dear. We are not that much different from them."

She hoped they would not be treated the way the beavers of Glendunny treated their Canuck cousins. That would be horrible. But what choice did she have? Glory looked at her pups now with a familiar warm glow in her eyes.

"Pups, we shall go forward with our heads held high in this wind-lashed river and with our mouths shut. You are swimmers now, dear ones. We shall fight our way down this river, crossing currents and finding the slipstreams that will boost our speed, the hidden underflows and back drafts that shall guide us true. You shall learn of the buried streams and eddies and all the forces of the river waters that will help speed us to the Across. We know the rivers and its ways like no other creatures. The rivers will protect us and help us as long as we are alert. As the birds know the winds, we know the rivers—the watery winds of this river and the ones to come, no matter if they are fresh or salt. We know the ways of these liquid winds."

And so after their rest in the muskrats' den, the little otter family with strong hearts slipped into the river again.

CHAPTER 22

Substitute Castor

Dunwattle *caught his breath as he saw Yrynn breaking through* a carpet of water lilies. He was so relieved. He had not seen her since she went into the cedar forest almost two days before. He had had nightmares of her being devoured by the Rar Wolves. But now there was her furry little face framed by two nymphas, the most beautiful water lilies of summer. The blossoms' pink color was so delicate, it seemed to go with her golden fur. He must write a poem—another poem. He had in those two days written perhaps a dozen poems to Yrynn.

"You're late, Yrynn!" A voice scratched the air. It belonged to Tonk, who was the substitute Castor this day, as Castor Feltch had to kit sit for her daughter.

"I was late too," Locksley piped up.

"I was too," Simon said. Then he flipped his tail and a glob of pond moss landed on Castor Tonk's head. Muffled giggles rippled through the assembled kits.

Good old Simon, thought Locksley.

"I wasn't late," Persil said. "I'm never late. But I've noticed that, like so many Canucks, Yrynn often—"

"Oh, go suck a rotten log, Persil," Simon replied, and his tail flipped another glob of mud that landed on Persil's head. Pandemonium broke out.

"Kits! Kits!" Castor Tonk was screeching now.

Suddenly the huge wing prints of Elsinore spread over Lower Scum. Silence fell on the pond as Elsinore landed. She turned her head toward the rebellious young beavers.

"Kits." Elsinore spoke in a low but penetrating voice. "The manner in which you treat substitute Castors is abominable."

The kits looked at each other. They didn't know the meaning of the word "abominable" but were fairly certain it was bad.

Dunwattle glanced at the swan. He felt something course through him. He loved Elsinore, admired her, and would never try to contradict her. But he felt compelled to defend poor Yrynn.

He lifted a paw from the water. "B-bu-but," he stammered. "There is something unfair here."

"And what might that be, Dunwattle?" Elsinore turned to him.

"It's unfair, and well, maybe it's a teensy bit abominable."

Elsinore opened her dark eyes wide. *Quite a vocabulary this one*, she thought. "Yes, go on," she said.

"Castor Tonk called out Yrynn for being late."

"Well, promptness is valued," Elsinore replied, and a smug look crossed Castor Tonk's face.

"Yes, but Simon and Locksley and I were all late too, and she didn't call us out."

"Well, you're not a Canuck," Retta whispered a bit loudly. There was a ripple of little giggles that passed through a half dozen of the beaver kits.

Elsinore seemed to swell. Her feathers plumped, and she batted the air, causing the still water to ruffle up.

"Now that is *abominable*, Retta. What you just said is positively abominable. In fact, it's indecorous, vulgar, common, rude, and unruly." Elsinore now swam over to Retta, who was cowering in the middle of a carpet of pond moss. "Part of my job as First Swan of this pond is to keep order. This was disorderly conduct. If this happens one more time, I shall have to report you to the Castorium." She then turned around and faced Tonk. "Castor Tonk, I think it would be very prudent, not to mention courteous, well-bred, and polite for you to explain that your remarks were not limited to Yrynn alone but were meant to include Dunwattle and

Locksley and Simon, since they were all late as well."

Castor Tonk appeared to hesitate. Elsinore paddled over to her. She wafted her wings slightly, and a clear message was sent to Tonk. Swans had incredibly strong wings that could knock a creature over, even break their backs. Yet at the same time this did not seem like an open threat. For Elsinore was cooing all the while in a voice the others could not hear. "You're a good Castor, Tonk. Well regarded, loyal. Do the right thing."

Tonk fidgeted a bit. "Er . . . uh . . . indeed. Dunwattle, Simon, Locksley . . . you three were all late as well. One more tardy mark and I shall have to tell your parents." Then she turned her head toward Yrynn, and in a hot, low whisper said, "Of course, you have no parents to tell."

There was an evil glitter in Tonk's eyes as she spoke, and Elsinore was tempted to smack her right there. One swift stroke of her wing . . . But she cut off the thought. She only whispered, "That was completely unnecessary. It was common." But this time, Elsinore did not utter all the other words that tumbled through her mind, like coarse, boorish, loutish, uncouth, and of course, just plain nasty. She would simply leave it at common. Had the old Aquarius been alive and presiding over the beavers, she would have reported this behavior of Tonk. But the new one, the Great Aquarius or His Eagerness, had proven himself just as common and vulgar as Tonk.

Yrynn's eyes were fastened on Dunwattle. She could not believe how he had stood up for her. No one had ever defended her or stood by her like that. Her parents would have, of course, but they had vanished so long ago and seemed to become dimmer and dimmer in her mind. Thinking of them just now made her think of the cedar forest, the Eyes of the Forest, and then her thoughts drifted to Lorna and the Belong. Yrynn thought, *How can I deny Lorna her Belong? When I stood in the cedar woods, it felt as though I were in my Belong—such peace. So how can I even think of not helping her to reach her Belong?*

Yrynn wondered if she might ask for Dunwattle's help in finding the Stone of Destiny. Then she could settle their bones so that Lorna and Fergus could get to their Belong at last.

CHAPTER 23

The Place
of the Bones

Glory had just caught a nice plump salmon, and the pups were being very helpful in dragging it to a low bank. They seemed to have matured so much in such a brief time, and now here they were in the lower Tweed. The scent of that river's water certainly confirmed the scent she had picked up on Dunwattle. Poor thing.

From this point in the river they would swim into a byway that would lead to the River Clyde and then straight into the Irish Sea. In that same instant that she was planning her path, there was suddenly an ear-piercing shriek. Her first thought was how big the mouth appeared and how long the teeth were. It was Grinfyll's mouth, and between his two fangs hung both her pups, Iggy and Edy. A gurgling sound came from the back of that horrid mouth, for after all, it must be hard speaking with two young otters in his teeth.

"Out with it, madame. The name!"

"Wh-wha-what name . . . ?"

"Don't toy with me. The name of the beaver that was seen."

She saw the fangs begin to sink into the fur of her cubs, into their throats. Something froze in her. She could not move. She could not breathe.

"Which one should I kill first? Choose!"

"Dunwattle!" she shrieked. "Dunwattle of Puddle-No-More."

In that same moment there was a great commotion. In a blade of moonlight, talons flashed as two eagles dive-bombed the lynx. There was a terrible screech. The pups fell from the lynx's mouth. Blood splattered the air. But it was not the pups' blood. It was the lynx's. The eagles had torn at Grinfyll's face with their sharp talons. He was blinded by his own blood. With her long tail, Glory swept the cubs into the river and steered them to the curling current.

"Heads up!" she cried out. She looked back to see if the pups were keeping up with her. Their eyes were glazed with fear, but they were swimming faster and stronger than they had ever before in their short lives. Glory vowed she would not go ashore until they reached the banks of the River

Clyde. And then somehow, some way, they would get to the Across and not rest until they had reached the other side. The journey might seem impossible. As impossible as swimming to the stars, but she knew it had been done before. How did she know this? Glory was uncertain. She just knew it.

There had been a time, her mother had told her—a time before time—when all the otters were one. There were no distinctions between river otters and sea otters. Glory sensed that this was so. She could not call it a memory, precisely, but perhaps a re-memory of that time when all otters were one. She must depend on instinct more than skill. This knowledge was raw and not simply learned. Glory felt that somewhere deep inside her this knowledge had lain in wait. Yes, it was just waiting. Waiting to understand—to comprehend this tangled history of her kind. For now she remembered what her mother called that time when all otters were one: the time of the mustah. There were no differences in that time between the waters—between rivers and seas, between clear and salt.

Dunwattle could hardly believe it. Yrynn had invited him to her den. She said she had something to show him. It would have been nicer if she had said she'd like him to come for tea. It was getting to be the season for lichen on birch or moss pudding. Lichen tea was such a yummy treat.

His own mum served it up beautifully in a hollowed-out burl cup, with a garnish of mint. But Yrynn had said only that she had something to show him and to come close to dawn, or the first pink, when the sky had just began to glow and most of the beavers of Glendunny would be sound asleep. He had considered bringing her some of the poems he had written. But every time he thought about it, he felt the fine hairs of his undercoat stiffening, which for beavers was the equivalent of blushing. Nevertheless, he swam toward Lower Scum, where most of the Canuck beavers lived. *Canuck*—the word rattled in his brain. He must stop using it, he admonished himself, as he took a deep dive into the front entry tunnel of Yrynn's den.

Seconds later he clambered into a small space where he could shake himself dry.

"That you, Dunwattle?" Yrynn's voice seeped down from above.

"Yes, sorry I'm late."

"You're early. It's barely first pink."

I'm eager, he thought. Then he thought of the G. A., His Eagerness, and felt another blushing sensation creep through his fine hairs. The very last creature he wanted to be like was that idiot G. A. On occasion he had even heard his parents whispering about how silly that beaver was. They of course were prejudiced. It had been expected that Wanda the Wattler, his mum's mum and his own grandmother, would be the next Aquarius. *But alas . . .* He cut off the thought. He could not bear to think of her horrific death at the claws of the lynx.

"Ah, here you are." Dunwattle sighed as he walked into a dining den that seemed aglow with the golden hues of her pelt. Who needed the colors of a breaking dawn when one was right here before his eyes? There was no tea service set out. No moss pad, no lichen on birch placed daintily on a plank of aspen with a garnish of fluffy mint moss. The space seemed to double as a sleeping and dining den. This was a rather bare-wood operation, as his father might have put it. In fact, the den was a mess. Yrynn was by no stretch of the imagination a good lodge keeper. But she had other attributes.

Yrynn seemed to sense him taking in his surroundings. "I know I'm not much of a lodge keeper."

"Well, you don't have a mum to teach you."

"You have a mum. Are you a good lodge keeper?"

"Uh, not really, I guess. But she taught my sister before she went off and started a family of her own."

"There you have it!" Yrynn replied with a hint of triumph in her voice.

"I have what?"

"It's always the females who are expected to do lodge keeping in addition to lodge building. Lodge building seems to be something both males and females do. But the neatness part, the organization, is always left to the females."

"Well . . . I . . . er . . . never thought of it that way."

"Hmmm . . . ," was all Yrynn replied.

But Dunwattle couldn't help but wonder if they were having a first fight. "I'm sorry if I offended you."

"Oh, no offense whatsoever. I just thought I'd point it out. But I didn't invite you over to discuss the merits of lodge keeping."

And obviously not invited for tea either, Dunwattle thought. No pudding. He had so hoped for that.

"I invited you over to meet someone."

"Really?" Dunwattle was slightly confused. He thought he knew every beaver in this pond. "Uh . . . who might that be?"

"It's a two-legs, actually. . . ."

The flash came back to him full force. The two-legs on the bank of the river. The blinding white blaze of light. The terrible twinge in his deep gut, in his skeat! And then the bespectacled two-legs peering down at him. *My! My! My! I can hardly believe my eyes. A beaver! A beaver in England!*

But how would Yrynn know? Dunwattle began to feel quite queasy and wobbled a bit. A dizziness overcame him, and he clamped his eyes shut. *I cannot throw up. . . . I simply cannot throw up.*

"Dunwattle! Dunwattle! Pull yourself together."

"You just told me you want me to meet a two-legs! How am I supposed to feel?"

"Calm down. It's not exactly a real two-legs."

"What in the name of Great Castor is a Not-Exactly-a-Real-Two-legs?"

"A ghost," Yrynn said softly. "And don't you start to wobble again. I won't have it!"

CHAPTER 24

Lorna
Explains

"**N**ow pull yourself together, Dunwattle," *Yrynn repeated.*

"Me pull myself together? What do you call this?" He nodded toward a pile of bones. Two-legs bones and a skull were heaped at the end of the bed of shredded bark and leaves in Yrynn's sleeping den.

"It just takes her a while to sort herself out, you know."

"No, I don't know," Dunwattle said. But in fact, he did recall when he first saw her on that night in the time of the Blood Moon. There had been a splintering sound as those long bones sorted themselves out. Of course he hadn't waited but blasted out of the lodge instead. He began to tremble as he watched this peculiar shuffling of bones. The knob of one bone would find the socket of another, and there was a tiny click as they locked together. Sometimes, however, there might be a mismatch between the joints—a knob might miss its socket. Dunwattle thought he heard, or maybe felt, the soft breeze of a sigh coming from the ghost, and then once he did hear the muttered words, *Not there, idiot, that's my elbow not my knee.... Fergus, that's your elbow!* Dunwattle himself was shaking. He felt Yrynn's paw pat him gently on the shoulder. Her paw was so comforting. Would he endure fear for love?

"Her name is Lorna," Yrynn explained. "It's a girl name."

He grew calmer and tipped his head as they watched the bones. "What's that thing that looks like . . . like a giant leaf or something wrapping around her?"

"It's a skirt. Clothes. You know two-legs have to wear clothes. They don't have fur."

Ahhh yes, he thought—the bright green skirt with the pictures of birds he now recalled seeing on the other two-legs. And of course, the queen's beautiful white satin gown from that picture. "What's that stuff all over it?" But then he realized he *had* seen the ghost's skirt before, when she had appeared in his own sleeping den and caused him to flee. But there had been other bones too. And then more recently there was a second time, but when the bones revisited him he had simply swooned. And when he came to, the bones and the strange mist that seemed to accompany them had vanished. Since then he had tried his best to forget it. Until Yrynn had so kindly brought the memory back!

"Blood. Lorna's blood. You know from the murder. Well, really it was a massacre."

Dunwattle now recalled Elsinore's own words as she had told the horrible story of Edward Longshanks. "She was murdered by Longshanks. Part of the massacre, wasn't she?"

"You know about that, Dunwattle?"

"Yes." He answered as if in a trance.

"How do you know?"

"The First Swan. Elsinore. But wait, who's Fergus?"

"Lorna's brother. You really scared him that night when she and Fergus came into your den."

"But why? How? How did you meet them, and why do you need my help?"

Yrynn crouched and drew her face very close to Dunwattle's. "To settle the bones, Dunwattle. To settle the bones."

"What? What bones?"

"Their bones—Lorna's and Fergus's."

There was a rustling. Dunwattle slid his eyes to one side and nodded in surprise.

"The bones, Yrynn, your friends. They have arrived, all of them."

"*That's yours, Fergus*, your elbow again." A whisper came

from Lorna, who had more or less assembled herself. "You keep losing it."

Then Dunwattle saw a bone from the pile float a short distance away. The knobbed top of the bone seemed to find its way into a socket of another bone and lock.

"Here we are! All together again," Lorna gasped merrily.

"Oh, this is terrific!" Yrynn exclaimed. "Her brother came too, Fergus. He's very shy."

"How old are they?" Dunwattle asked.

"Very." She paused. "Very very old. Like almost a thousand years old."

"Great Castor, Yrynn!"

Yrynn almost hissed at him now. "That's the tragedy. Don't you understand? They were murdered. Murdered when they were just . . . Well, Lorna was just short of her first double-digit birthday."

"Ten? You mean ten?"

"Yes, but my brother, Fergus, was already twelve."

Dunwattle blinked. *Can this be? Am I actually talking to a ghost, a haint?* The voice was like sand. Sand shifting beneath rock, just like when they excavated for the foundations of their lodges.

"Hi," a shy voice said.

"Fergus, this is Yrynn, and this is Yrynn's friend Dunwattle, who I think can help us. Help us find the stone, the Stone of Destiny, and settle our bones."

"What?" Dunwattle asked. "A stone? And settling bones? They do seem a little"—he was grasping for a word—"a little restless."

Yrynn turned to Dunwattle. "I was going to explain, but you . . . you almost fainted before I could tell you. This is the good part."

The good part? Dunwattle fervently hoped that some good part was coming.

Together Yrynn and Lorna began explain.

Yrynn began. "You see, Dunwattle, these two kits—I mean children—they have gone a-wander."

"A-wander? But that only happens to beavers who die. Whose bones never settle, who can't find the Great Pond. My mum feels that Grandma might have gone a-wander. She told me after Wanda was murdered that Mum feared she might be lost on her way to the Great Pond. So, you mean it can happen with two-legs as well?"

There was a tiny sniffle that seemed to come from Lorna, but her nose bones were so tiny, it was hard to tell. "Yes, it can," she whispered. "You know, Dunwattle, you might be an animal and I am a two-legs, as you say, but our lives are over. We want to go to our heaven, Neamorra, but we can't get there until our bones are settled. Until then we are doomed to wander forever in this sad in-between place, this nowhere . . . this place we call feasghair."

Yrynn turned to Dunwattle. "Do you understand now, Dunwattle?"

There were tears in his eyes. "Yes, I think I do." He was thinking of Wanda. There had been nothing left of her except for a couple of teeth. No bones, not a tuft of fur, even. "I heard my mum and da talking about it." It had been past his bedtime, but his mum was moaning, *Oh, Grizzmore, will Wanda ever get to the Great Pond?*

"And if they don't get to the Great Pond?" Lorna asked. "Where do they go?"

"The myrk," Dunwattle whispered. Then he slowly turned to Yrynn. "Do you ever worry about your parents, Yrynn? Because when they disappeared, no bones were ever found."

Yrynn was unsure how to answer his question. She missed them terribly and had been lonely, but she had never wondered about their unsettled bones. She was unsure how to respond to Dunwattle's question, but she decided she must answer truthfully. She shook her head slowly. "I miss them. I miss them fiercely, but for some reason I just know they made it . . . made it to the Great Pond and were not sucked into the myrk."

"The myrk?" Fergus asked.

"The in-between place, like your feasghair." Yrynn replied.

When they were done, Yrynn took a deep breath and Lorna's ribs, that were now all in order, appeared to expand a bit and take something like a breath as well.

"So there you have it, Dunwattle," Yrynn said. "If you can help us find the stone, the bones of all these people massacred by King Edward Longshanks, they will settle again. They became disturbed, shaken by the earthquake, but they will settle again. The bones will settle. . . ."

The bones will settle. The words rang in Dunwattle's head. He looked at the two ghosts, Lorna and her brother, Fergus. They made for odd beings—a curious kind of life-form. The bones were visible but sheathed in a shroud of mist that made the sister and brother appear slightly transparent. Gossamer creatures, they were. Both had a cloud of soft russet colors around their heads that he guessed was their hair, not fur. Yes, they had learned from Castor Helfenbunn in Two-legs Vigilance class that human beings had hair on their heads that they could wear in different styles.

He recalled everything now that Elsinore had told them. The king called Edward Longshanks and the reason the Castors had come and made this pond here. For they knew no two-legs, pardon, no humans would come near it. Now he knew. *It truly is haunted.*

Yes, I must help them!

And in that very same moment an idea came to him. "Locksley!" he murmured.

"What's that?" Lorna and Fergus both spoke at once.

"I'll help, but you must allow me to bring my best friend."

"Who's that?" Yrynn asked.

"Locksley of Was Heath. I promise you, Locksley will come if I ask him."

"Well, good luck," Yrynn said. Dunwattle could tell that Yrynn didn't think he could convince him. But he took no umbrage at this. Indeed, he felt sorry for Yrynn. She really didn't know what it was like to have a true friend.

CHAPTER 25

X

"*Oh my ... my ... my ... what happened to you, my friend? Good-*
ness gracious, you're almost as ugly as I am." The old
beaver walked closer to Grinfyll. They were in their usual
meeting place far from the pond. The lynx's face was a
bloody mess. One eyelid had been ripped off completely. An
ear hung in shreds. "Aren't you a pretty sight!"

"No worse than you!"

"Do you have my information?"

"Not until you respect me!"

"I'll respect you when you tell me what you promised."

"Respect me first!"

X shrugged. "All right, pretty is as pretty does." And

with that he slapped the lynx with his powerful tail. It would be several minutes until Grinfyll regained consciousness.

When he did open his eyes, it was like a bad dream. The disfigured face of X hung over him. The bulbous growth blossomed like a monstrous flower. His other eye, the one that was not obscured, glared with a mad light.

"Dunwattle!" Grinfyll gasped. "Dunwattle of Puddle-No-More."

"Good. Excellent, my young friend." He paused dramatically. "Did you know that I have the blood of a maranth in me?"

"No," gasped Grinfyll.

"Ah yes."

"I'd heard the Canuck kit has maranth blood," said Grinfyll.

"Believe me, she's not bright enough to be a maranth. But for my purposes it might prove convenient that the others think she is one."

"Huh?" Grinfyll blinked in confusion.

"'Huh,' the lynx says! Like the ignoramus he is. Now how can I respect a fool like Grinfyll?" He waddled off and called over his shoulder. "I have some business to attend to. Politics, you know."

"Pol-i-what?" said Grinfyll.

At this, X burst into gales of laughter. The laughter scraped in Grinfyll's ears like sharp stones.

Meanwhile Dunwattle made his way from Lower Scum to the far eastern end of the pond in the region known as Was Heath. This was the lodge of Locksley's family. He entered through a back entrance and went directly to Locksley's sleeping den.

"Dunwattle, what are you doing here at this time of the morning?"

"Are your parents here?"

"Yes of course. They're sleeping."

"Good." He looked about and gave a big sigh.

"They're sound asleep. Sleeping like logs. You know that's a two-legs expression? Weird, right?"

"Yes, I guess so."

"What's bothering you? You looked worried." *So would you, Locksley,* he wanted to say. *Brace yourself.* How to begin? *I want you to meet some dead people, dead two-legs. Well, ghosts, really. They want us to help them with something.* That didn't seem quite right. "Just follow me, Locksley."

"Follow you where?"

"To Lower Scum, Yrynn's lodge."

"I knew it! I knew it! You kind of like her, don't you? She is cute. I admit that. A bit on the quiet side."

"Just shut up, Locksley. It's nothing like that." He scowled. Locksley would be the last creature in the world to whom he would admit his feelings for Yrynn. It would result in endless teasing.

They left the lodge and swam together quietly to Lower Scum. Entering through the back tunnel they continued up into Yrynn's sleeping den, where she and the ghosts of Lorna and her brother, Fergus, waited. Dunwattle turned to his best friend and rested his paw lightly on Locksley's shoulder. He could feel his best friend trembling. He could sense the stiffness in Locksley's under pelt bristling up in fear as his eyes settled on the two ghosts. Their slightly transparent, tattered clothing hung on their bones. Then Dunwattle began to speak.

"Lorna, Fergus, this is my best friend, Locksley. Locksley of Was Heath."

"Oh, the Heath . . . ," Lorna said wistfully. She turned slightly to her brother. "Fergus, remember the Heath? We used to go out there around the holiday, Michaelmas Day. That really is when the heather is at its best. Oh yes, we'd pick heather. You cannot imagine how many different colors of heather there are: purple, of course, and frail pinks and the bold, bright yellows. Chapel bells we called the—"

Fergus sighed. "Lorna, stop."

"Oh, sorry," she said as she clamped a pale hand over her

mouth as if ashamed. But her eyes turned up and twinkled as though she was smiling.

Are her eyes really blue? Locksley wondered. Was it possible for any creature to have blue eyes?

"That was BW," Dunwattle said in a low voice.

"BW? I don't quite understand," Fergus said.

"Before Water." Locksley continued, "Before there was this pond, the land was very different, with meadows and heaths and moors. Then the beavers came and changed the landscape by cutting trees and damming streams. What had once upon a time been a heath or a meadow sank away into the depths of the pond, along with your village. Our pond seems to have drowned your village. Well, our ancestors created it. That's what beavers do. We flood land. We build walls of wood and rock and mud that hold back water and we create ponds and wetlands. We build lodges to live in. So before there was water, or BW here, there was a village and then Longshanks arrived and the . . . the . . ."

"Massacre," Lorna said softly.

"Yes, the massacre." Locksley continued, "And the founding beavers of this pond probably knew that this would be a perfect place to build a secret village of their own. So, they made the pond of Glendunny. It erased the horror of the Longshanks massacre. But not completely, because other two-legs knew about it and feared it was haunted."

"But then the earthquake happened," Yrynn added.

"That is what stirred the bones."

A silence filled the lodge of Yrynn. Then she and Lorna tipped their heads and looked at Dunwattle and Locksley, not uttering a word. They both seemed to say, *Shall we go and settle these bones?*

CHAPTER 26

"It's a Matter of Vysculf"

E lsinore *had seen from a distance Snert of the Snout approaching* the G. A.'s lodge, just as he rounded the bend out of the lower Snout. Snert was a quiet, elderly beaver. He kept to his own. And although he was in the Castorium, he rarely spoke up. His disfigurement, Elsinore thought, perhaps caused him to be somewhat reticent. He was, however, an excellent dam builder. No one really understood the engineering and the architecture of a dam better than Snert. For these abilities alone he had become a member of the Castorium at a fairly early age. He just seemed to have a gift for grasping architectural structure and detecting leakage. It was as if he could see immediately where the leak was and its cause.

There was, however, one thing that slightly annoyed Elsinore about this beaver: it was that she sometimes caught just a hint of perhaps false modesty and beneath that was perhaps a deep well of arrogance. He would often begin his critique of a dam project with the words, "Well, I'm not an expert, mind you, but I would suggest if you dive to the grid work you might find the problem." Inevitably his suggestions worked. "It's a miracle," someone would say. "Snert, you were absolutely correct in your analysis! We should call you Snert the Miracle Worker!"

Elsinore watched now as Snert of the Snout approached the G. A.'s lodge.

"Who goes there?" Hobbs, His Eagerness's servant, called out.

"'Tis me, Snert of the Snout."

"And what may I ask is your business with His Eagerness?"

"It's a matter of vysculf."

Elsinore felt her gizzard crinkle. *Great Cygnus! Someone knows.*

"Vysculf!" Snert said louder.

"Oh! Oh dear!" Hobbs gasped.

Elsinore had to think fast. Did Snert know who was seen? If so, she must warn Dunwattle. And what would that stupid old fool the G. A. do? She must remain calm. Stay very still in her nest and press her ear to the listening hole she had made in the bottom—there she could hear into the main chamber of the G. A.'s lodge. This was a secret of the swans that none of the previous Aquariuses knew about. But it was essential—essential to the well-being of the pond. The secret had been passed down through the generations of First Swans who had preceded her.

"And they say, Your Eagerness—" The words of Snert floated up through the hole.

"Who says?"

"I am sorry, Your Eagerness, I cannot disclose my sources at this point. But my sources say that Dunwattle of Puddle-No-More was seen on the lower Tweed."

Elsinore dared not breathe as the words trickled into her ear.

"I myself feel that as soon as possible there must be a meeting called of the Castorium."

"Yes, yes of course . . . but . . ."

"But what, Your Eagerness?"

"I must of course be prepared."

"What do you mean? Have I not prepared you enough?" There was a slight tone of resentment in Snert's voice, a definite pout.

"I must be appropriately dressed for the occasion. Hobbs! Oh, Hobbs! The green velvet cape. The tiara or my crown? Which shall it be? Well, whatever, let's add a sprig or two of fern fronds to it—give it a little . . . a little . . . Oh stinko, what's the word? Elsinore?" His Eagerness screeched.

"Yes, yes . . . Yes, Your Eagerness," she replied. "Coming!"

Elsinore descended from her perch to the rooftop of the lodge. "You called?"

"What's that word I'm looking for when I decorate my crown . . . when I want to give it a little . . ."

"Pizzazz?"

"That's it, pizzazz! Yes, pizzazz. Dear Hobbs, can you find me a few fern sprigs?"

"I suppose so, Your Eagerness." He sighed wearily.

"Oh, do you think that it might be a little much if I wear that wig you found for me on your most recent trip, Elsinore?"

"Perhaps, Your Eagerness."

The beaver sighed. "But honestly, Elsinore, Much is More and More is Much, so why not wear it?"

Elsinore at this point sent up a silent prayer to Cygnus. Scavenging for the G. A. would give her time to warn Dunwattle.

Seconds later Elsinore had lifted off and was flying toward the Dunwattle family lodge near Puddle-No-More. She prayed that Dunwattle was home, but that his parents, Berta and Grizzmore, were not yet back from their Chomp on Dam 5. But such was not the case.

"Sorry, dear," Berta said to Elsinore. "He's still out with

Locksley. These young'uns, you know. They can work all night and then still have enough energy to fiddle around in the dawn. You could check up in Was Heath at Locksley's place."

"Actually, dear"—Grizzmore, Dunwattle's father, poked his head up through a roof vent—"I think I saw him heading toward Lower Scum."

"Oh dear." Berta sighed. "Why would he go down there? There's no class down there today with Castor Feltch."

"No idea," Grizzmore replied. "But I have to be on my way. Just got the signal that the Castorium is gathering. So, we'd both better go." Elsinore's gizzard again flinched. She clamped her eyes shut. *The poor fellow. If he only knew the trouble their son was in!*

Within seconds Elsinore was winging her way toward Lower Scum. But Lower Scum was still as could be. She paddled around to several lodges, poked her beak into the various gaps in the walls, "yoo-hooing," as it were, to see if anyone was awake. But she was greeted only by the great chittering sound of the snores of beavers in deep slumber. There was one lodge that must have been completely empty, for she did not even hear the slumbering snores. She believed it was that of the young beaver who had been orphaned some time ago, several months before the earthquake. At this point she supposed that all she could do was return to her nest and make sure her listening holes were clear of any debris for the meeting of the Castorium.

Within the next few minutes, the pond began to stir with the dozen beavers, the members of the Castorium, as they plied their way to the lodge of the G. A. Soon Elsinore was hearing every word all too clearly. Castors Feltch and Tonk were arguing, even though not all the members had arrived yet.

"This is ridiculous. The kit did not do this on purpose," Feltch was arguing.

"Dunwattle must be made an example of. This kind of behavior cannot be tolerated," Castor Tonk was saying. Elsinore's gizzard twisted painfully as she saw Dunwattle's father approaching from one end of the pond and none other than Locksley's mother and father from the other end.

"If he has been seen, it will be the death of us all . . . ," Snert intoned in a doleful voice. "We have lived here peaceably for centuries now. They will try and track him and find him here. They must not track him to Glendunny."

"But how would they, Snert?" Castor Elwyn asked.

"They have their devices, these two-legs. The scent can be carried on water. The waters of the lower Tweed where he was apparently seen—"

Castor Elwyn cut him off. "Those waters flow to the Irish Sea eventually through a latticework of streams and creeks. There are waterfalls and pitch shoots between here and the Tweed, no two-legs could possibly track the scent back to Glendunny. They aren't like otters, for goodness' sake."

"We don't know, Castor Elwyn. We don't know," Snert said ominously. "Do you want to risk all of our safety because of one foolish young beaver?" Snert was prepared to argue and argue hard. The present Aquarius was in no way up to this challenge. If he failed, Snert would step into the position. He had come so close in the last election. Wanda of course had won. Then this fool, Oscar of Was Meadow, was second—only beating out Snert because he was younger. Snert was next in line now.

"Now here, here!" he heard Grizzmore grumble loudly.

"Just what are you suggesting, Snert?" Castor Feltch said, barely concealing her anger.

"I am suggesting an elimination plan."

"That is no solution!" Castor Brora rumbled.

"It's the only solution," Snert rasped. "We need the lynx."

Dunwattle's mother stood up on her hind legs. "You are going to set a curse of lynx on our son? *Our son?* Whose grandmother was destroyed by a curse of lynx? How dare you?"

"How dare I? I am a true patriot of this pond, ma'am. I am the chief engineer. I have presided over every dam built here in the last decade. And now your son has caused a leak in our dam of secrecy."

"Stop right there!" Elsinore squawked down. A hush fell through the lodge.

"That's Elsinore." The G. A. gasped.

Now Elsinore had to think quickly. She began batting her wings as if she had just landed.

"Hobbs! Hobbs!" Elsinore squawked again.

The old beaver Hobbs tottered to the top of the logs and looked straight up. "Great Castor, Elsinore. What is it?"

"Tell His Eagerness there is a Code Five alert."

"What in the name of Avalinda is that?" Hobbs asked. "Code Five, what is it?"

"Never you mind. Just tell His Eagerness."

Code 5 had been invented by Elsinore and the G. A. to signal that there might be a royal accoutrement—a sword, a royal sash with medals—that the swan had glimpsed and might be retrieved. Elsinore had also suggested that they should not speak so publicly of the G. A.'s obsessions, and hence they should have a code system by which they could communicate when certain royal trappings, bit and pieces were found. She felt she was doing the ridiculous beaver a favor. Although she was unsure why she would go to such lengths. She supposed it was all part of her peacekeeping efforts. The rest of the beavers did not need to know any more than they already knew of their leader's vanities and silly preoccupations.

In another minute, the G. A. himself exited the lodge

and climbed atop the roof to confer with the swan.

"Is it true? Code Five!"

"I do believe so. Perhaps a scepter. Also, another cloak." Elsinore was making this up as she went along, but she'd figure out something. The cloak would be the easy part. She could snatch anything from a clothesline. And somehow, some way, find a scepter-like item.

"I should dismiss this meeting immediately. What excuse should I give? I can't say Code Five."

"No, no. You can't say Code Five. Uh, tell them it's a Code Ten. Yes, of course: that's the code for forest fire. Tell them I spotted a possible forest fire on my dawn flyover. And they need to be ready to make a clear-cut break. All Chomps must go . . . er . . ." She tried to think of a reason. "Uh . . . because a wind shift is expected that would push the fire closer to Glendunny. All those trees to the east, just beyond Was Meadow, must come down. They have to get out there and start chomping." Was Meadow was actually where the G. A. had lived before taking lodge at New Fosters. It was the center of his family's lodges. This would all make sense. The G. A. would not want his home scorched by fire.

"Oh, go quickly! And, Elsinore, dear servant, I so want a scepter. There is a decision that must be made soon, a very important one. And I feel that for my full authority to be honored, I need to hold a scepter while announcing the decision."

"Yes, a scepter. I'll do my best to get the one that I spied on flyover." She sighed. But in truth she did not know what she was doing. If she could find Dunwattle, maybe she could warn him. Save him somehow. He was not full grown but just halfway grown. He might weigh as much as twenty pounds—could she possibly transport him? And to where? Well, out of England, she supposed. Maybe just across the channel.

Vysculf! Oh, how she wished she'd never heard the word. And how did Snert know? That was the strangest thing. She would have to think about that.

CHAPTER 27

Feasghair

The three beavers—*Dunwattle, Locksley, and Yrynn*—began to walk with their two-leg friends Lorna and Fergus. They felt as if they were descending, and yet they found themselves in a place that was not water, nor mud, nor air. It was simply mist. Their paws felt nothing beneath them and yet they did not slide or fall.

"What is this? The . . . the Belong?" Dunwattle asked.

"Oh no." Fergus, who had become slightly more talkative, now spoke up. "This is the between place. The feasghair, we call it. You see all the bones?"

And as soon as Fergus said the word *bones*, they saw them. Some seemed to float in the mist. Others were gathered in piles.

"But how will we ever find the Stone of Destiny?" Dunwattle asked. He looked at Yrynn, and she gave him a look as if to say, *How should I know?* He turned to Lorna. "Where was it last seen?"

"Well, no one really saw it because it was buried, hidden in the crypt of the church that held the bones of the old monks. It was a good hiding place, the elders thought. No one would go around digging into old graves. But now everything here is a graveyard. There are bones everyplace."

"The church, that's the first place we looked," Fergus added. "But we've picked through every single bone there. Not a stone—at least not one the size of the Stone of Destiny."

"How will we know it if we do see it?" Yrynn asked. "One stone looks like another."

"Oh, you will know it. It's a dressed stone, carved so it could fit into the seat of a throne. There were also some designs carved into it. Emblems and things. And it has an iron ring at each end and is slightly scooped on top to fit . . . to fit . . . a king's bottom. He had kind of a big butt, King Alexander did. Or so they say. He was long before our time," Lorna said, and giggled. Her giggles clinked in the air like tiny bells.

Locksley looked at her. He was charmed by everything she said or did. There could not be a more appealing, more enchanting two-legs—even if she was not quite all there, more of a skeleton loosely gathered into the shape of a body.

They continued walking through the slowly swirling mists. There were tumbled-down cottages and split skulls, and in certain parts of the village the mists were tinged a ruddy color, as if still stained by the blood.

"I . . . I . . . I'm not sure how to ask this," Locksley began. "But have you found any bones belonging to your family?"

Lorna stopped. She put her hand into what seemed to be a pocket in her skirt. "I think," she said slowly, "this might have been a bone from our baby sister, Adair." She shook her head sorrowfully. "I'm not sure. I . . . I just had this feeling. I keep it close to me, because if we do settle the bones, if we do get to the Belong, I want to keep her close."

The three beavers were shaken. Each one resolved to try to help the sister and brother. Their grief was almost unimaginable. These children were almost living and yet they were in the land of the dead. This was feasghair, and they must help these children reach the Belong. They moved on through the wreckage of the village. The bones that swirled in the strange mists were stained with the blood from long ago.

Locksley had no notion of where they were in relation to the pond. They must be beneath it—but were they in Lower Scum, where they had set out from Yrynn's lodge?

Or could they be in his neighborhood of Was Heath, or Dunwattle's Puddle-No-More? Maybe even far east in Was Meadow? He might as well be blind, turned upside down, and swimming through a night sky of dim stars. Time and distance meant nothing here in the feasghair. Time and distance were unhinged from the universe that they knew, from any universe they could imagine.

But just then there was a sound—not an unfamiliar sound but that of beavers squabbling. Were they near a dam? Often when working on dam repairs, Chomps would begin arguing heatedly about the best way to work, whether to use alder or birch for the warp of the wattling mud. The biggest arguments usually involved those on the "diversion" Chomps, about how to change the course of a stream to lessen the water flow pressure. That's what hydrology was—the science of the movement of water over the land, any kind of water—creeks, streams, oceans, all of it. And indeed, it was Castor Elwyn, their hydrology teacher, whose voice seemed to ring out now, but it was not about water! Normally a soft-spoken, even-tempered beaver, he was distinctly agitated.

"This is intolerable, outrageous. . . . You are proposing a curse be set upon this poor young beaver?"

Tonk interrupted. "It will be the end of our community, our pond, our world if . . . if . . . This is *vysculf* we're talking about. The culprit must be eliminated."

Locksley turned to look at Dunwattle.

Yrynn stepped forward and reached out with her paw to touch Dunwattle's shoulder. "You've been seen, haven't you?" Dunwattle nodded but said nothing. "I'll stay . . . stay with you, Dunwattle."

"And so shall I," Locksley said.

"What are you talking about?" Lorna asked. Dunwattle took a deep breath. He knew he must be honest. "Lorna, the first time I saw you . . . when you appeared in my sleep chamber, I was frightened. So frightened that I bolted. Bolted right over Dam Eight and swam as I've never swum before, into a place I had never been. And when I reached a river, I was seen."

"Seen?" Fergus asked.

"Seen by a two-legs. I mean a human being. You must understand that a beaver has not been seen in this land for more than five hundred years. We must keep our existence a secret. It is the Secret of Glendunny."

"But why?" Fergus asked.

"Because," Locksley added, "if we're seen, the two-legs will kill us. Kill us for our fur. Our pelts are very valuable."

"But you can't stay here . . . here in feasghair," Lorna said fiercely. "Feasghair is nowhere. It's not for the living like you. You're not dead. It's not heaven or earth. It's the In-Between for the dead."

"But where is it, exactly? Where are we?" Locksley

persisted. "Are we in the pond, beneath it? In the air? Above the earth?"

Lorna scratched the thin mist of her red hair that hovered over her skull. "You see, my friends, it is not here. It is not there. It's not now or then or when. I suppose you might call this either Was Pond or Not Quite Earth But Never Heaven. We are in the shadowlands, and that after all is what feasghair means—a shadowy place. You know how butterflies begin as caterpillars suspended in their cocoons until they transform into butterflies? Finally they each hatch out of the cocoon and begin a new life with wings and beautiful colors. Well, we are trapped in this cocoon known as feasghair. It's as if our wings have been torn off. We are nowhere, but we can still hear the There."

"The There? You mean the world above you. The pond and all of us," Dunwattle whispered.

Lorna nodded.

"Then kill me, Lorna!" he pleaded. "I'd rather be killed by you than a . . . a curse of lynx! Like the one that killed my grandmother."

"I shall not!" She paused. "You have absolutely lost your mind." Her blue eyes glittered. "If I kill you, then I shall go to hell and never get to the Belong!"

Meanwhile, far to the south of Glendunny, Elsinore was winging her way toward one of her favorite royal dumps near the River Dee, where the queen's summer palace was in Aberdeenshire. So far, in spite of her despair she felt from the discussion in the Castorium, it had been a successful trip. Nevertheless she was far from happy. Anything she could do that might delay the G. A. calling for a resumption of the meeting to vote on the curse of lynx was good. And the G. A. was still waiting for the delivery of a scepter and cloak from her before taking this crucial vote.

In the meantime, Elsinore had found a quite royal-looking, purple bathrobe that she snatched off a clothesline while flying over Aberdeen. Now for the scepter. Of course, not a real scepter but something she could pass off as one. She soon spotted a cluster of dumpsters behind a municipal building. She might as well have a look.

But just as she was flying over the lower Tweed, Elsinore noticed out of the corner of her eye an odd object. It was black and quite shiny. It was not a bird. It was not a living creature at all but a spider-shaped device. Elsinore had in her long life and hundreds of thousands of leagues flown during the course of that life encountered many airborne objects in the sky, ranging from weather balloons to airplanes and the peculiar devices known as blimps. Blimps were nonrigid airships that lifted into flight by the pressure of gas. The blimps were used largely as flying billboards to advertise events. When the Olympics had been held in London, Elsinore almost had to stop flying during the summer as the sky was so crowded with the beastly devices.

But this object she now spied was much smaller and emitted a high-pitch whine that scratched her gizzard. Elsinore, a good-tempered swan rarely given to harsh language, now swore in the oath of the devil swan. "What in the name of Uff is going on?" Uffern, swan hell, was Uff's domain. She didn't like the looks of this. She began a deceptive maneuver of flying in rising double eights maneuvers, and on the third of the double eights she dissolved in a cumulous cloud.

"Damn! Damn Damn!" Adelaide McPhee slammed the palm of her hand down on the desk. "It's gone; the swan's gone," she muttered at the large monitor. Huddled behind her stood half a dozen graduate students who had joined Operation Castor. All were peering at the screen. "How much battery power does Lucy have left, Mark?" Adelaide McPhee asked.

"Five percent. Enough to get home if we bring her back now." Lucy was the name the research team had given to the drone. The drone had been named for Lucy Woodridge, one of the first female graduates of New Cavendish University and who had been made a dame of the British Empire for her work on the scavenging activities of porcupine. "But if the swan emerges from those clouds and continues on the course it had been on, Lucy won't make it back." The young man looked up mournfully as he spoke these words. Adelaide groaned.

"I have got to raise enough money for at least a second drone. Somehow, some way." She wondered if she could squeeze any more out of her great-aunt Glencora in Peebles, whom she had been visiting at the time of her sighting of the beaver. If they had three drones, they could send them out separately. Three eyes on the sky would be better than one. And if they didn't launch them from Fife but from Peebles instead, they would be closer to where she had first spotted the beaver.

Adelaide McPhee's aunt Glencora was very wealthy and lived in a large house on the banks of the lower Tweed. It slowly dawned on her that indeed that was where their base of operations should be! Why had she never thought of it before? An idea began to form in her mind. Suppose she could move the whole team to Peebles? There were a dozen in all, but Aunt Glencora's house would accommodate at least six, maybe eight of them, and then there were bed-and-breakfasts in the town and Airbnbs. And then the best idea of all came to her. They had never named this beaver, but suppose they named it Glencora? Even though it most likely was male. If they named it after her great-aunt, who was a passionate environmentalist, she might perhaps donate more money to the research. She had so much money. She hardly knew what to do with it.

Adelaide had been so excited when the swan had drifted into Lucy's camera field. Her students did not at first comprehend her excitement. "I'm sorry," she apologized. "I should have explained. You see, swans are known to often take up habitation in beaver ponds. A very good example of what biologists call a symbiotic relationship between different species. Benefits both. The swans become part of the beaver community. And what do those graceful and gorgeous white-befeathered creatures have in common with those chunky, waddling beavers? Well, I'll tell you: pond food! Swans love the algae and all the aquatic plants. They often build their nests on abandoned old structures of beavers or muskrats. The swans might look upon beavers as furry little farmers. For, with their creations of ponds, they cultivate the most scrumptious algae and weeds that the swans feast on. So if we can track this swan, we might find our beaver."

But the team of young scientists led by the fearless Adelaide McPhee couldn't track Elsinore now—not yet. As Lucy's batteries were sputtering out, Elsinore remained firmly tucked into a thick layer of cumulous clouds. After twenty minutes she finally emerged from the cloud cover. By then she barely heard the whine of the eye in the sky, as it had retreated to the east.

Swans' hearing, as that of other birds, was vastly superior to the hearing of humans. This gave them an enormous advantage in terms of navigation. They used this ability with a combination of other factors, such as the earth's magnetic field, of course the sun and the stars, and their keen perception of light to guide them. Swans, like other birds, can perceive wavelengths of light that humans never can. And because of this they are superb navigators in many difficult conditions that might challenge ordinary human beings. So Elsinore emerged not lost at all. She resumed her flight when she dropped out of the clouds far to the south of Glendunny and on track for one of her favorite places near the River Dee, where she had first spotted the cluster of dumpsters.

Angling her wings, she began her descent. Her heart sank a bit as she alighted on the edge of the first dumpster. "Hard trash," she muttered. It must be a renovation. Nevertheless, she tiptoed over the contents of the first dumpster. Broken window fans and old air-conditioning units. Pipes and more pipes. *Could a pipe serve as a scepter?* Showerheads and toilets, and then she spied something more. It was a stick with a large rubber thing on the top, almost like a dome. It looked brand-new. Indeed, there was a tag attached. She twisted her head around to read the tag. *Mr. Clean 440436 Turbo Toilet Plunger £6. Not bad,* Elsinore thought. Now what exactly was this used for? Obviously something to do with a toilet—she flipped over the tag, which gave a brief description.

**Turbo plunger has rubber-grip handle and extended
rubber plunger, provides highly effective results**
Caddy has a nonslip base
Handle Length: 14 1/2 inch; Cup Size: 4 3/4 inch

Well, why not a scepter? Easy to grip, light, impressive length. And that long beautifully turned wooden stick with the "rubber-grip handle," whatever that was? She narrowed her eyes. Actually very useful. The G. A. could simply hold it or wear it. The rubber dome was almost like a two-legs hat of some sort and most likely waterproof. Swimwear!

CHAPTER 28

His Eagerness and the Toilet Plunger

W hen the Grand Aquarius caught sight in the distance of Elsinore returning with what looked like a bountiful haul of royal treasures, he could barely restrain himself. Within minutes of her landing, Elsinore had squashed herself and the treasures into the G. A.'s receiving chamber.

"Is the Castorium still in recess?"

"Of course. We cannot proceed with our discussion or a ruling if I do not have my scepter." His eyes seemed to feast on the toilet plunger. "That's it, isn't it?" He hardly seemed aware of the purple bathrobe.

"Indeed. It is the finest. French, actually." Elsinore tapped the attached tag and removed it. "Mr. Clean Turbo Plunger, it says here. That's just a rough translation from the

French. In French the words are more . . . how shall I say? Mellifluous? It translates from 'Le Plongeur de la Toilette.' It was from the palace of Louis the Fourteenth. I've told you about him?"

"The one they called the Sun King, right?"

"Yes indeed. Now the wonderful thing about this is that it's . . . Well, how should I explain?" Elsinore paused and half shut her eyes as if she were reflecting deeply. "This instrument is really a dual action . . . er, pardon me. Dual purpose, I should say. It can function as a scepter or . . ." She paused dramatically.

"Or?" the G. A. asked.

"Or serve as a crown—a waterproof one. Why not try it on for size?"

Elsinore helped fit the plunger on the G. A.'s head. There was a little sucking sound as she pressed down on the rubber dome. "Perfect fit."

"Yes, I do think so. And when I'm on my throne, won't I look grand!"

"Oh, you will, Your Eagerness! And where is your throne right now?"

"It's in the Castorium, of course. I always have my footmen move it there from the receiving chamber when the Castorium is in session. And it's been freshly relined with moss. Much more comfortable to sit in, and this fresh summer moss is so plentiful now."

"Yes, yes, Your Eagerness." Elsinore then paused. Could she say anything that might influence the G. A.'s mind? To dissuade him from this reckless course of action—the summoning of a curse of lynx—that now threatened to kill Dunwattle. The swan thought back on the reflections she had been recording in her diary about this beaver monarch. How in such a relatively brief time this once-modest beaver, Oscar of Was Meadow, had changed so drastically. Had he perhaps accidentally imbibed some stink water? In some cases, the stink water caused delusions. But never delusions of grandeur. More often terror and ongoing, uninterrupted nightmares. But those symptoms usually subsided in a very few days. There could have possibly been some stink water released around the time of the earthquake, but why would the G. A. be the only one to experience it?

"Sir, I mean Your Eagerness, I am touched that you are so appreciative of my humble offerings to you."

"Humble? Elsinore, dear swan, they are hardly humble. These gifts you bring me are royal, imperial, regal. . . ." Indeed, Elsinore marveled that the G. A. had at least glanced at the special word book she had brought him. The thesaurus, as it was called. It listed all the other words that had the same meaning for the one word you knew. "And what you brought me today, the scepter and the cloak, in royal purple, no less . . . The fabric—what did you call it? It's not velvet but feels softer."

"Terry cloth, sir."

"Terry cloth," he said dreamily. "The words even sound soft."

"Well, Your Eagerness, I have a request."

"Certainly, dear Elsinore. What might you request?"

"As you know sir, I come from a very long line of First Swans for beaver ponds, going back to the time of Great Fosters. Now I am concerned about this vysculf situation. And the implications concerning the young kit Dunwattle of Puddle-No-More."

"Yes, Dunwattle comes from such a fine family. And you know his grandmother was killed by . . . Well, dare I speak the word?"

But Elsinore did. "Lynx—a curse of lynx. And I am afraid that the Castorium might be considering the aid of the lynx to destroy Dunwattle." She now took a deep breath. "Lynx are savage killers."

"Why ever would the Castorium do that?" the G. A. mused. A veil of confusion seemed to drop over his eyes. "Why, Elsinore? Why?" His voice trembled. For some reason this gave Elsinore hope.

"Yes indeed, why?" She paused a moment. "So, what I am asking is that you permit me to attend the session. I mean, I assume that you are ready to meet with them again, now that you have your scepter."

"Yes, yes, of course." The G. A. reached out and touched

the scepter gently, almost reverently.

"Then may I attend the Castorium meeting with you, as perhaps your minister?"

"Minister?"

"Yes, minister. Remember I told you how reigning monarchs have ministers who help them with policies and rules of governing. I know the members of the Castorium are in that sense ministers. But perhaps I could serve as your prime minister of . . . of security. Since I am already charged with flying out to make sure our pond is secure from . . . any two-legs intervention." Elsinore's mind was racing. She was making all this up as she went along. Of course, much of this was based on truth, as part of her job as First Swan was the security of the pond.

His Eagerness blinked rapidly. His eyes seemed to clear and appeared brighter than ever.

"Of course! Yes, come along." He rose and waddled off.

"Don't you want Hobbs to announce you? Do the 'Hear Ye, Hear Ye'?"

"Nonsense, this is an emergency."

Elsinore was stunned. This was extremely clear thinking for the Aquarius.

"Follow me, Swan!" He looked over his shoulder. Any trace of his outrageous vanity seemed to have vanished. The G. A.'s eyes were lucid, seemingly cleared from any delusions or illusions of grandeur. There was a fierce set to his powerful jaws. What a Chomper he had been in his day, thought Elsinore. Oscar of Was Meadow could tear his way through the hardest of hardwood trees in a flash.

She accompanied the G. A. down a long winding passage that led into the circular chamber of the Castoria Castorium. She followed with hope in the wake of his terry cloth robe and the scepter he clutched in his mouth.

"All rise, the Grand Aquarius is here," Hobbs announced.

The G. A. seemed confused as to why they were all standing on their hind paws for him. He quickly scrambled up onto the throne that now had been lined with the softest of moss and clover from the woodlands edging the pond. He looked out at the sixteen assembled beavers. Then he glanced down at his scepter and blinked a bit.

"Aren't I a lucky monarch? This is my new scepter. Our dear Elsinore found this for me. It's French. In French they call it a 'Plongeur de la Toilette.' Right, Elsinore?"

Elsinore was aghast. She'd had such hope. When they left the receiving chamber, he had seemed so clearheaded and clear-eyed, and now in a matter of seconds he was droning on about the toilet plunger and the royal-purple terry cloth bathrobe. What in the name of Uffern had happened? Elsinore felt in this moment that she was at the gates of swan hell. *I might be in the lodge of beavers, but this is Uffer!*

Little did she suspect that the Grand Aquarius himself was feeling a bit odd at this point as he looked out upon the beavers of the Castorium. He was in fact a bit confused as to whether he should be holding the scepter or wearing it on his head as a crown. For as Elsinore had explained, it was dual purpose. And why couldn't he remember the part about the turbo action? Was the plunger scepter made from terry cloth or was that the royal robes? Despite the thick pouf of moss and that of the royal robe, the throne never seemed to quite fit his bottom. So uncomfortable. *Damn this throne!* he thought.

CHAPTER 29

When Legends
Come True

If I kill you, then I shall go to hell and never get to the Belong. Lorna's words were still ringing in Dunwattle's ears.

"If this is feasghair, the shadowlands, which shadows are we near? Because I hear voices arguing. Live voices of live beavers," Locksley said. "Are we directly below the Grand Aquarius's lodge?"

"More likely just beneath the chamber of the council, of the Castorium, in the lodge." Dunwattle sighed. "Of all the routes we could have taken, how did we wind up here? Yrynn, you were in the lead when we left, weren't you?"

This was the question she had been dreading. "Uh . . . uh . . . er . . ."

"What is it, Yrynn?"

"This is hard to explain, but I actually thought I saw another . . . another ghost here in feasghair, and I was sort of following it."

"Who?" Fergus and Lorna both blurted out.

"Mum or Da?" Fergus said.

"Baby Adair?" Lorna looked as if she might be crying—crying blue tears.

"No." Yrynn shook her head solemnly. "Not a two-legs. Not a human, I mean."

"Then what?" Fergus said.

"A wolf pup. I think it was a wolf pup that led us here."

"Bones? Fur?" Fergus asked.

"Well, not exactly. Not really a human but misty in the same way you are and a little transparent so I could see the bones. It's as if they were floating about in a thin cloud but definitely in the shape of . . . of . . . a wolf pup." Yrynn's heart beat faster. She could hardly believe what she had been seeing, or almost seeing, at this moment.

Locksley took a step closer to her. "But Yrynn, have you ever in your life seen a wolf, let alone a wolf pup? Is it a Rar Wolf?"

"I'm not sure. But I've been to the cedar forest where they are said to live, and I've only felt a kindliness there in those woods. I even felt as if it were a blessed placed. A kind of Belong."

"But you aren't dead," Lorna whispered.

"True," Yrynn replied softly. Not dead at all, for at that moment she felt something soft and furry brush against her legs. "My, my," she sighed. "Look who's here." They all gasped as now they saw it too. A silvery little wolf was tumbling around Yrynn's legs. She ran her nose through its fur. "So soft." The pup nuzzled against Yrynn's side now. *Follow me*, the pup seemed to say. When she shook, the silvery fur appeared to radiate a tinge of blue. The others began to see the little creature as well.

It can't be, Yrynn thought. But she didn't want to say anything. Not yet. "We must follow this pup," Yrynn said, trying very hard to keep her voice steady.

And so, they all began to follow in the paw prints of the frolicking pup.

"She's walking in circles," Locksley said.

It was in fact like circles, but with each circle the circumference grew tighter and the sound of the arguing in the Castorium grew louder, until they heard the Grand Aquarius bellowing. "Stop it! Stop it!" There was a loud crack that sounded like wood breaking on stone. They all looked up.

"Now you've made me break my scepter . . . my . . . my Plongeur de la Toilette!"

The three beavers; Lorna; her brother, Fergus; and the little wolf pup all tipped their heads up. There was something about the sound of that crack. The ghosts and the beavers all looked at each other.

It's the Stone! The scepter broke on the Stone of Destiny!

Of course, they didn't know that it was the handle of a toilet plunger that had broken. But they all knew the sound of wood cracking on rock.

The little pup looked at the creatures surrounding her and wagged its tail happily.

"Now take my bones back!" she barked.

"Back where?" asked Yrynn. Something was stirring in her own mind. Was the legend coming true? The legend of Little Blue and Little Kit?

And Little Kit—who was Little Kit? Yrynn hadn't thought she had spoken aloud but the air suddenly seemed to ripple with tiny giggles.

"You!" The wolf pup spoke softly. "You are Little Kit, the star kit, a spirit kit who goes with me through the night during both winter and summer. But it is now in the Moon of the Callow Ferns that we draw the closest. The words of the Spirit Legend streamed through Yrynn's mind. *Back to the cedar forest they must go. Take them when the Little Wolf constellation rises in the night. Take them when you can see the brightest of those stars in the tail star, Stellamara.*

"Stellamara." Yrynn whispered the word in astonishment. But it wasn't just a word. It was a name.

"That's me!" The wolf pup was baying now. But it was not the yapping and baying of the pup she was hearing but the echo of her own mum's voice telling her the stories. *"Once upon a time, in the great North Woods of Canada, there was a beaver kit and a little wolf pup who had wandered afar from their lodge in the sky. . . ."*

Stellamara! The name exploded in Yrynn's head. The lost name she had been searching for since her mum and da had vanished.

"Yes, Stellamara. For that is who I am, the lost star that was said to have fallen into the sea. And so I am blue—blue as the sea. The pup of the chieftain. I shall be in my Belong."

And Little Kit—who was Little Kit? Yrynn hadn't thought she had spoken aloud, but the air suddenly seemed to ripple with tiny giggles. "You!" Stellamara spoke softly. "You are Little Kit, the star kit, a spirit kit."

Yrynn could not believe it. She felt a happiness flood through her. She thought they were just stories, legends. *But maybe, just maybe, sometimes legends can come true!*

A soft breeze blew behind them, and another shape melted out of the swirling mists. "It's . . . it's . . . a Castor," Locksley whispered.

"Not just a Castor," Dunwattle said. His voice was full of wonder. "It's . . . it's my grandmother Wanda—Wanda the Wattler."

"Wanda the Wattler, the Aquarius . . ." Locksley seemed to choke. "The Aquarius that never . . ."

"Take my bones too . . . ," the shape whispered.

The shape was becoming clearer and more distinct to Dunwattle. Could it be? It was! "But I can see you, Grammy, just as I can see the pup Stellamara."

"It was all the lynx left." The voice was that of Wanda the Wattler.

But as Dunwattle spoke, the misty forms—that of the wolf pup and that of Wanda—began to dissolve. All that was left were two small piles of bones. And the echo of those voices. *Take my bones. . . . Take my bones. . . .*

The two ghost children and the three beavers looked at each other. Each felt a mixture of dismay and hope. How would they do this? How would they take those bones out of these shadowlands to their own Belongs, whether called Neamorra or the Great Pond, no matter what? Names did not matter any longer. Belonging was what mattered.

CHAPTER 30

A Wrapped Riddle

Hours later, in the last sliver of moonlight that fell directly on her diary, Elsinore began to write. It seemed as if the clouds were accommodating her so she could finish these thoughts. A phrase had come back to her like a distant echo. . . . *A riddle wrapped in a mystery inside an enigma.* Where had she heard that phrase? She could not recall, but the words seemed to describe His Eagerness, the Grand Aquarius. When Elsinore thought about this beaver once known as Oscar of Was Meadow, he had been a modest fellow. Self-effacing. A good, industrious soul—that was one of the finest things one could say about a beaver. An excellent bark stripper. Not brilliant nor imaginative, but bark strippers seldom were. Nevertheless, his estimates on the swelling rate of any log in any temperature of water were always precise. He was not gifted with the engineering genius of, say, Snert of the Snout. Not a "Miracle Worker."

So, with these thoughts in mind Elsinore began to write. And as she began to write, she realized that in some way she was suspicious of miracle workers. They could, after all, be no better than tricksters. Tricksters with devilish designs. Or worse yet, conspiracy mongers trading in lies and subterfuge to trap innocent creatures. Elsinore remembered the Shyvana legends that told of the trickster swans. Clever, deceitful, and full of evil.

No miracle worker, our Oscar, but perhaps the victim of a misguided miracle. What happened to this simple fellow? Elsinore thought.

For the official installment of a new Aquarius, the custom is to wait for the first night of a new moon. That would have been several days after Wanda's death. But nonetheless Oscar had assumed the duties of the Aquarius for a week before the earthquake occurred. And in the brief period following the quake, Oscar was a model of effectiveness—assessing the damage to lodges, storage chambers, and dams. Dispatching Chomps for repairs and keeping spirits up. The damage to New Fosters, the very heart of our pond and seat of our governing body, the chamber of the council of the Castorium, was severe and added to the delay in the ceremonies for our

new Aquarius. But during that time Oscar had made a fine
leader.

It was soon after, once the restoration of the circular
chamber of the Castorium had been finished, that Oscar
began to change. The place was a mess from the earthquake.
Two weeks of wattling and plastering with the deep mud,
what Elwyn began to call "cataclysmic" rock. Such rock had
been brought up by the convulsions of the earth, littering the
chamber and needed to be removed or rearranged.

Elsinore inhaled sharply. "By Cygnus, that's it!" she muttered.

Elsinore now recalled the stone, the one that Oscar of
Was Meadow had been drawn to, that was chiseled so carefully as if to fit the butt of a two-legs. She knew now in a
split second that the stone must have some sort of powers.
It was enchanted. A blight had been cast on that stone,
a malediction, an evil eye on any creature who sat on it,
except the rightful one. And Oscar of Was Meadow *was not*
the one! It was not for creatures like Oscar but for two-legs!

At the same time, almost the very moment that Elsinore
began to realize the truth of that stone, the Grand Aquarius
himself, now alone in the Castorium, slipped off the throne
to relieve his discomfort. He blinked several times. *Why is*

it, he thought, *that I feel so much better off the throne than on it?* Why had he never realized this before? By way of experimentation he tried this several more times. Each time he was off the stone, he experienced a sense of relief. He felt more himself. The world seemed clearer to him. And yet he had spent so much time on his throne. He had always insisted that it be moved every time he moved. From the Castorium, to his den, to his receiving chamber, his sleeping chamber, his dining den, his study. He was always sitting on it except when he slept. And now that he thought about it, sleep had been his only time of complete peace. He stared at the throne and backed away from it several feet. With each paw step back, with each inch, he felt better. And questions began to float through his mind. *I do not feel grand at all. . . . Why is that? But I actually feel good. . . . Why am I carrying this silly-looking thing called a scepter . . . and wearing this royal robe? Why do creatures call me His Eagerness or the Grand Aquarius? I don't feel royal. . . . I feel silly. I should be the Castor Aquarius. Not the Grand Aquarius. Not His Eagerness.*

Castor Aquarius, he thought. That was a dignified title, a worthy title of a good and responsible steward of a vast pond. The leader of a keystone species, as all beavers had been since time immemorial, who with their superb engineering skills had built dams, walls of wood, mud, and rock that held back water and created ponds and wetlands.

Beavers! We shape continents! What a silly fool I am. I have been bewitched! And there are those who have taken advantage of me!

Was it too late? There was a knock on the post outside his entry. "Your Eagerness!"

"Yes, Hobbs?"

"Snert of the Snout is here and wishes a private audience."

"Really?" He blinked. He felt something stir deep in his skeat. He was not quite prepared to see anyone at this moment of stunning clarity. He looked at the throne.

"Yes, really," Hobbs said, wondering why the master would question him like this.

"A moment, please. I am slightly indisposed." He glanced at not just the throne but the scepter, the purple robe. Should he appear in his royal raiment? Why might Snert seek an audience with him anyhow? Something stirred in his memory—oh yes, it was about Dunwattle of Puddle-No-More. Vysculf and lynx . . . a curse of lynx. His eyes opened wide in horror. Had he actually agreed to this ridiculous proposal? Had the Castorium voted for it? He couldn't remember. Every time he sat on that dumb, accursed throne, his mind became foggy. Should he sit on it now for his audience with Snert? But then his mind would turn foggy again. He could not decide what to do.

"Show him in, Hobbs."

Snert crawled in with his eyes cast down. The brilliant engineer went through an elaborate protocol of silly postures and formalities that Oscar had dreamed up after glancing at a royal etiquette book that Elsinore had brought back from one of her flights. "Gestures of Obeisance," the chapter had been called. His Eagerness had loved it. Practically memorized the chapter word for word, but Oscar now felt a profound embarrassment from his skeat to his gullet. It was like trying to digest worm-infested wood. Snert had mastered these poses and postures. He was a model of obsequiousness, a master of submission, groveling there on the floor. It was nauseating to watch and yet Oscar had to.

When the groveling finished, Snert finally raised his head. "Oh!" he said. "I expected you to be on your throne."

"Uh, just a lower back problem . . . It is not . . . er . . . the most comfortable seat for me right now."

"I'd be happy to send out some of the members of my Chomp to bring in some sponge moss to line it with."

"Don't bother." Oscar was now examining Snert more closely. He had always been so impressed with this beaver—the genius engineer. The Miracle Worker, some called him. There was no doubt that he was a genius, but now Oscar regarded him with this new clarity he had been blessed with since he moved off his throne. There was something else lurking behind Snert's dark eyes. There was intrigue brewing. Oscar felt certain of this.

"And what is the occasion for this visit?"

"You don't recall?" A new brightness seemed to illuminate Snert's eyes. Oscar caught it immediately. *He is almost pleased that I don't recall.*

"Go on, refresh my memory."

"The vote on dispatching the lynx curse was a tie. It would of course be up to you to decide in such a situation by an order, a decree."

A dreadfulness began to creep through Oscar. It rose like foul water in his gut. "Oh yes." His voice had withered to a mere whisper.

"I think I have additional evidence against Dunwattle."

"Really, now?" Oscar's voice was stronger. He kept his eyes fastened on Snert. *This fella is up to something.*

"I feel he has been consorting with the young orphan beaver Yrynn."

"So?"

"Yrynn, the one rumored to be a maranth—a witch."

Oscar cocked his head and studied the beaver, who now seemed slightly nervous. *He comes to me with what he calls evidence. "I feel," he says. Feeling is not evidence, nor is rumor.* Hadn't there been some maranth witch talk before the murder of Wanda the Wattler, the true inheritor of the Castorship? It was of course nonsense. Wanda herself was not simply a genius in her own right, but a model of honesty, kindness, and compassion. Was that why Oscar himself felt undeserving of this office? It was perhaps why he had felt that he could never measure up to Wanda the Wattler. Who could? Was that why he had furnished himself with all these empty symbols of power? *I am truly a fraud!* The knowledge dawned on him like a blast, like a tectonic event, like an earthquake! But at the same time Oscar knew instantly that he must play these next few minutes very carefully.

"I feel that what you offer as evidence must be explored further."

"Why?"

"Why, you ask?" He now regarded Snert with narrowed eyes.

"Sorry, Your Eagerness. I did not intend to be rude."

"Of course not," Oscar said amiably. "I would never suspect our most brilliant engineer of being rude. I just need more time for reflection. Dismissed."

Snert blinked. He hadn't expected to be sent off so quickly. He had prepared an entire argument to push for invoking the lynx. But Oscar simply stared at him, then gave a curt nod as if to say, *Get on with it.* So Snert dropped to his knees and backed out of the chamber.

As soon as Snert of the Snout had left, Oscar turned and charged the throne with all his might. There was the sound of a rupture, then a rumble, as the wood below the chamber floor seemed to break. At that moment the stone dropped and the lodge of the Castor Aquarius seemed to shift on its foundations. However, the lodge still stood and so did Oscar, formerly of Was Meadow. But now as he glimpsed himself in the fragment of a gilt-framed mirror that Elsinore had brought him, he almost did not recognize the reflection that peered back at him. His Burger King crown had slipped over one eye. He was clutching an odd object with a rubber dome at the end of a stick of some sort. The single eye he could see appeared bleary, not with fatigue but confusion. *Who am I? Who was I? Who am I supposed to be?*

CHAPTER 31

To the Belong

The kits—*Dunwattle, Locksley and Yrynn—as well as the* two-legs children Lorna and Fergus stared at the thick swirls of mist at their feet. They had heard the noise from above and felt the reverberations but did not know what had just occurred.

Finally Yrynn said, "I don't think it's another earthquake."

"No!" Fergus exclaimed. "Not at all."

Then Lorna burst into tears. "It's here. Somewhere very close. I know it. I just know it. We must find it." She wheeled about. "Dunwattle, you go that way." With one of her bony fingers she pointed. "And you . . . you, Locksley, go the other way."

"But Lorna," Locksley said. "There are rocks all over here and bones and skulls—how will we know which rock is the Stone of Destiny?"

"You'll know it . . . you'll"—Lorna was stammering—"you'll feel it."

"Lorna." Dunwattle now spoke up. "You're a two-legs; you're human. You might feel such things in a different way from us. We're beavers, Castors."

Lorna turned now to Yrynn. The little ghost pup was snuggled against her fur. "Not Yrynn."

"What do you mean, Lorna?" Yrynn asked.

"You're different, Yrynn. You feel many things. Just look at that little wolf pup, Stellamara. I believe you can cross between worlds, between creatures with four legs and two legs, animals and humans. The stories you told me about Little Blue—look, they are true. The legend is true!"

As she was listening to Lorna, Yrynn experienced an odd sensation that she could not quite believe. But she felt a tiny pink tongue licking her paw.

Lorna said, "See, here is Little Blue, Stellamara, fallen just as you told in the story. From the sky to the sea and now here . . . here in the In-Between." She spoke softly. "Neither heaven nor hell. Just the In-Between, where some souls wander forever. My brother and I are so tired of wandering. Find the stone and the gap between Neamorra and feasghair will close."

"And," said Yrynn. "you shall belong? Be in the Belong?"

"Yes," Lorna said, and it seemed as if an actual tear dropped from her eye. But could bones cry?

Yrynn's eyes rested on that tear and then she saw another and another. She took a step forward. There was a path. A sparkling path through these mists of feasghair, illuminated by tears, drops of tears. The path glowed more intensely. And she began to realize that, in fact, she herself could traverse two worlds—not of the Belong or feasghair but those of earth and spirit, pond and stars. She was of the legends. She was a spirit kit.

And ahead she saw something dark that was flecked with bright silvery specks.

Yrynn turned around and faced the others. "I found it," she said quietly. "I found the Stone of Destiny. The true seat of kings and queens."

Lorna and Fergus ran up to her. The two children almost seemed to be breathing now, breathing as their silvery tears fell down onto the stone.

"Neamorra!" Fergus said. "We're so close."

"Yes, we can go now to the Belong," Lorna whispered and took her brother's hand. Their bony fingers intertwined.

"I . . . I . . . ," Dunwattle stammered. "I don't understand."

Lorna turned to him in her tattered skirt. "You don't need to understand, Dunwattle. But you helped us."

"I did nothing."

"You and your friends did everything," Fergus replied.

"What? What did I do?" Dunwattle asked.

"You listened to us and you listened to your friend Yrynn. You brought your friend Locksley. You believed in us. You came with us."

"That's all someone needs sometimes . . . just a friend," Fergus said. "With a friend you can become more. You can become braver, smarter . . . just better."

"But we're not even your kind," Dunwattle said.

"What does it matter what kind you are?" Lorna said.

A creaking voice now rose from the small pile of bones next to those of the wolf pup. Dunwattle felt a shiver run through him. It was Grammy Wanda. "Listen to her, Dunwattle. Now it is your time to take us to the cedar forest. Creath Malach."

"Creath Malach?" whispered Yrynn.

Dunwattle turned to his grammy. "Creath Malach, that is the true name of the cedar forest?"

"Indeed, dear." The bones of his grammy stirred a bit. "It means, 'All Souls.' It is the Belong for us, for non-two-legs. For all of us. It really doesn't matter what you call it. It just is what you feel the Belong is. It's all the same in the end. Creath Malach, the Great Pond, Neamorra. Heaven."

For a pile of bones, the voice of Wanda was becoming quite chatty as she began to sort herself out. "As Elsinore told me once . . . what's in a name? She is so well-read, that swan. It came from a play. I think." She paused and scratched her bony skull, which seemed bereft of any fur. It was as if the kits were looking straight into Wanda's mind as she continued with her thought. "'What's in a name? That which we call a rose by any other name would smell as sweet . . . ,'" Wanda the Wattler uttered in a soft voice.

The three kits carefully picked up the bones of Wanda and the wolf pup. Lorna had found a satchel for them. Then they all stood together, rather awkwardly, for the last time.

"It's . . . it's time to say goodbye," Fergus said.

"Yes, I suppose so," Locksley replied. His eyes were focused on Lorna—she after all was the first two-legs he had ever seen or met. Even though she was a ghost, he was nevertheless surprised that he had such deep feelings for her. A sadness began to creep through him. He was trying to imagine her as a beaver. Could a beaver have blue eyes? Could a pelt be red and blow freely around like this . . . this thing called hair? But it was not just her hair or her eyes. Her bones, so long and graceful, seemed to glow through the mist of her skin. Locksley watched as her shape moved on. How lovely those bones were, and he thought, *What a fine life I have had . . . for I have known a human, a girl lovely in her bones. And when she moved, there appeared to be music within her soul.*

And then Lorna and Fergus were gone. Like two evening stars they faded into a new morning that was their Belong.

Quietly the three kits made their way back, not to Yrynn's lodge but to another that she knew about in Lower Scum where they could hide away.

"No one ever comes here to this old lodge. Supposedly there's a stink water spring. So don't try and drink anything." Yrynn now turned to Dunwattle and Locksley. "We have done a good thing," she said softly. "The two-legs bones are back in their place, their Belong. But there is still work to be done. These bones"—she peered at the satchel in her paws—"the ones of your grandmother Wanda and the little pup Stellamara, the wandering one of the wolf constellation, those bones must be settled as well."

"But how? When?" Locksley said.

"When the blue star rises, the star of Stellamara."

She patted the bag with the bones of the little wolf pup and Wanda. "But," she continued, "the wolf constellation rises in a few days, toward the end of this moon, the time of the fireflies and the water striders."

"But we can't go out at night," Locksley said. "That is when all the Chomps are out working. They'll see us!"

"And they'll hunt me down!" Dunwattle said in a low voice. "You heard Snert talking about the curse of lynx when we were down there in the In-Between place, feasghair. We could hear every word of the talk in the Castorium."

"We don't have to go at night," Yrynn said.

Dunwattle and Locksley looked at each other in confusion.

"But here we can't see the stars hidden away. How would we see the Little Blue star?" Dunwattle said.

Yrynn seemed to roll her eyes at their ignorance. "Look, we don't have to see it to know that it's there. The constellations rise in the east and then by morning they have slipped to another day, away from the one here in our pond. We just have to know that it is the time the blue star is rising. You can believe without seeing. Have faith. And it's almost that time of the summer when we'll be able to see it clearly as soon as it starts to rise. We don't even have to go outside yet to find it. We can peek through the wattling."

"And we'll see it then?" Locksley said.

"We'll see its reflection in the pond. That is what's so wonderful about dark water. It becomes a mirror for a world we might not be able to see," Yrynn said, then added, "And then in the morning when the beavers of the pond sleep, we'll go with the bones to the cedar forest."

"All right," Locksley said. "Sounds . . . sounds possible," he replied hesitantly.

It might sound possible, Dunwattle thought, but he had flinched a bit when he heard Yrynn say those words *We'll go with the bones to the cedar forest.* He remembered back to that time when he had watched her walk into those woods. It was almost as if she were drawn by a magical force. But what about him? He was still going to be hunted. Was that the choice—hunted or haunted? Some choice!

The three beavers guarded the bones and kept a watch on the sky through the reflections in the pond. It was almost that time, the time of the Wolf Moon, when the blue star would begin to rise. The very next evening Yrynn felt her heart skip a beat as she saw quivering on the black surface of the water the reflection of the bright blue light of the star Stellamara. The Wolf Moon had come and Stellamara had risen—finally!

Yrynn slid down an interior tunnel to the dining den, where Dunwattle and Locksley were munching as quietly as possibly on old rotten wood. Not the tastiest. Rotten wood made for belches and gaseous emissions that beavers called bletches. Until he had met Yrynn, Dunwattle had never hesitated to let loose with a bletch. In fact, he and Locksley often had bletching contests, with points given for the loudest and the smelliest. But since Yrynn had entered his life, he had tried to suppress these urges. They were no longer so much fun. Maybe he was growing up.

Yrynn poked her head in. "The blue has risen!"

"Stellamara?" both Dunwattle and Locksley said.

She nodded. "We go tomorrow well after dawn. After first pink. In the long gray it will be safest." The long gray was those hours after the full black of night and the first pink of the dawn. It was during this time when the pond reverberated, not with the chomping of beavers cutting wood but the sounds of their snores, thick snores issuing forth and hanging over the still water of the pond like a sonorous cloud of exhalations—the sounds of beavers sleeping. The hours when the beavers finally ceased their relentless industry and sank into dreams of succulent wood and weed and still water.

CHAPTER 32

The Lady Glencora of Skibodeen

ar from Glendunny on the grand estate of Skibodeen, Glencora Barrington settled into her favorite chair in her library and took out the Henry Bates Gilmore book on the flight paths of migrating arctic terns. They were a most amazing species of birds that migrated from pole to pole each year, twenty-five thousand miles in all. If Lady Glencora were to return in a second life, she would have perhaps wanted to come back as a tern. She had not ever gone very far from England, really. But she had no real complaints. How could she? Her world really was this house, this estate, and perhaps most of all, this splendid yet very cozy room lined with oak bookcases, ornate carpets, and volume upon volume of wonderful books.

The ceiling was domed, and at each end was a crescent-shaped window with stained glass depicting a bird. In the east-facing window, a swan, and in the west-facing one, a spotted owl. Glencora Barrington was an "amateur" ornithologist. She was always careful to say "amateur," seeing as she had no advanced degree in the bird science of ornithology. Therefore, she most often called herself simply a bird lover. And as such she had ascended to become the president of the Protection of Birds Society of her county in Scotland. She was also a member of BEPA—British Environmental Protection Agency.

She of course had been excited to learn that her niece Adelaide had in fact all the academic degrees that she herself had long craved but did not have. Glencora herself was over ninety and grew up in an era when too much knowledge in a young woman was frowned upon. Excessive intellect was considered a kind of deformity to the feminine nature. Good marriages were all that young women were expected to graduate to. And she had made a very good marriage to a very rich and very kind—but not especially bright—man. She loved him, but even he, Charles Barrington, became slightly nervous when she had become a member of BEPA. "It's so public, Glencora!" he had exclaimed.

"Of course it's public. How else are we going to accomplish anything without being public about it?"

"But it's so easy for such movements to become vulgar and tip into radicalism."

"There is nothing vulgar or radical, Charles, about clean air, clean water, and the preservation of wildlife."

He gave in. He often gave in to his wife. He regretted that they had not been able to have children, for then instead of lavishing all this attention on endangered species, she would have been distracted from such public endeavors. But he was a gentle man, an agreeable man, and he seemed to know that his wife was a bit smarter than he was. To humor her he had often given her beautiful paintings of birds or other bird art; thus, the stained-glass crescent windows of the swan and the owl had come to be in their library. He had also given her several paintings by the famous American artist and ornithologist John James Audubon. They were massively expensive and so exquisite. But she dared not tell her husband that they absolutely revolted her. For poor Charles did not know that Mr. Audubon painted from death, not life. The painter killed more than four hundred birds of different species to immortalize them. She had sold all of them immediately following Charles's death and given all the money to BEPA.

"Auntie! Auntie! It's here." Adelaide McPhee burst into her aunt Glencora's library. Her cheeks flushed with excitement.

"Oh, the zone! The zone!"

"Drone, Auntie. Drone not zone." She giggled. "Or phone, as you called it the other day."

"A sibling for Lucy. How lovely!"

"And guess what we're going to name it?"

"What?"

"Glencora!"

"Oh, how kind! I don't know if I'm worthy of the honor. I mean, you can't really compare me to Lucy Woodridge."

"Of course I can, and you're way more political."

Glencora rolled her eyes. "Glad your uncle Charles can't hear that. Or at least I hope he can't." She pointed one finger toward the ceiling. "He'd be turning in his grave.

"Now are all your researchers happy at the B and B?"

"Oh yes, Auntie." Adelaide plopped down next to her in a chair and took her hand. "Let's hope the swan appears again and maybe can lead us right to the pond where this beaver came from."

"Yes, yes. It's rather nice thinking that there might be a secret community of beavers in Scotland and maybe close to our own county here in Peeblesshire. They're good creatures. I actually proposed that we award them the coveted species of the year award from BEPA because of their work in preserving wetlands." Glencora sighed.

"It would be lovely if we could put a GPS device on it," Adelaide said.

Auntie Glencora blinked at her niece. "A what on what?"

"A GPS. You know, Aunt Glencora. A global positioning system. It's a device that you can fit right on the swan's ankle, or on any creature, for that matter."

Oh dear! Glencora thought. Although it had been said that upping swans in no way injures the creatures, Glencora recalled in an article she had read someplace that somehow it could affect their nesting and egg laying. She hoped she hadn't gotten herself into something unforeseen, as she didn't like the idea one bit of some gadget, some electronic device attached to any bird's ankle. She'd heard of criminals after they had been released on bail from jail having such devices attached to their ankles, but swans weren't criminals. And once a person attached one to a swan, why not just go ahead and attach it to some wandering beaver who swam down the Tweed? *Oh dear . . . oh dear.* What had she gotten herself into? It sounded too much like spying. And that was a world she had put behind her—far behind her, decades ago during World War Two.

CHAPTER 33

In the Shadow of Shame

"*Forget it, Hobbs. I'm going in. Announced or not.*" Elsinore *swept* the elderly beaver aside with her wing. She had heard the entire exchange and rushed down as soon as Snert left.

"You heard?" the G. A. asked.

"Yes, Your Eagerness—"

"Just Oscar, please, just Oscar," he replied, holding the broken plunger limply in one paw.

"I heard everything, Oscar."

The beaver clamped his eyes shut. "I am so . . . so ashamed. It's as if I have lost my senses entirely."

Elsinore looked about the den. "Where is your throne?"

"Gone and good riddance. I kicked it through the floor. It's sunk to the bottom of the pond." Once more Oscar shut his eyes tight, as if trying to recall something. "I don't want to say I wasn't responsible, but I . . . I . . . ," he stammered. "I think that throne . . ." Again he hesitated, for what seemed like a long time. "I think that throne was in some way bewitched. Although I don't want to use the word. Let's just say it was not made for a beaver. Not a Castor Aquarius. Not for any beaver. It was made for a two-legs. A two-legs king or queen."

"Enough of that. You have simply awakened and seen the light, Oscar."

"Some light. Did you hear what Snert said about Dunwattle and Yrynn? He wants to set a curse of lynx on both of them. He said Yrynn is a maranth."

"I heard it all," the swan replied.

"Elsinore, are you thinking what I'm thinking?"

"I am indeed. I think Snert has been consorting with lynx for a long time. I think he planned the murder of Wanda so he could be the Aquarius of the pond."

She paused. "Now how do we stop him from murdering Dunwattle?"

Elsinore twisted her neck into what appeared to be an uncomfortable position, with her head tucked partway beneath her shoulder feathers. Her voice was slightly muffled. Oscar had to take a step closer to hear. "There is an old saying. I must have read it in a two-legs book," she said as she now untucked her head from her favorite thinking posture.

"What might that be?"

"Give a man enough rope and he'll hang himself."

"But Snert is not a man, not a two-legs."

"I have a feeling these words of wisdom cross species. Castor, human, or swan, they still apply."

"Perhaps. But how do you suggest giving him enough of this thing called rope?"

"Well, I'm speaking metaphorically, of course. You don't actually need a rope. Let Snert go on believing you are still in this . . . How shall I call it? Still in this imperial fog of grandeur and monarchy."

"But the throne is gone! Gone forever! I never want to see it again."

"But you have your scepter."

Oscar glanced at it as if it were the most disgusting thing on earth.

"And there are the crowns I got you, the ones from King Burger. There must be at least twenty left."

Oscar sighed. "And to think I actually considered changing my title to King Burger of Glendunny pond."

"Well, I talked you out of that good and fast, if you remember," Elsinore said.

"Thank you, Elsinore," Oscar said softly. "I am so sorry."

"No time for remorse now. You must go on playing your part. Even though I know it will be painful."

"But how do we catch him? How do we stop him in

this . . . this dastardly plot?"

"Let me think about it."

"I just wish there was some way we could warn the kits to stay out of sight."

A new light flashed in Elsinore's eyes. Was it possible that the kits sensed this and had made themselves scarce? She had not seen any of them going off to Chomps last evening. Quite unusual. She could only hope that they had somehow become aware of the danger Dunwattle was in.

It was just after dawn when Elsinore left Oscar, throneless but calmer than when she had arrived. She had to convince him to keep "the stupid scepter" and the King Burger crown, just for appearances' sake. No one at this point should know that Oscar had come out of his royal dreams. "Be mindful, Oscar. This is war. We don't know who we can trust. Elwyn, we can trust for sure, as well as Feltch, but Tonk? I'm not so sure. Even Helfenbunn raises doubts in me. And Carrick as well. He can on occasion prove troublesome, like his daughter, Retta."

"So what do we do?"

"We keep a sharp lookout for Dunwattle and Yrynn and Locksley, for a start."

"And I am to play my part. But aside from the scepter and the silly crown, what do I do?"

"For now, nothing more than that. I just need to do

a few more flyovers. I need to ascertain where the lynx congregate. How they plan these attacks, like the one on Wanda. But I do know this: they seem to prefer high ground. They killed Wanda on high ground, about as close as they ever get to the cedar woods." She didn't mention that she was worried that she had not seen Dunwattle or Locksley for almost two days. It worried her. But she did not want to share this with Oscar, not yet.

"Ahh . . . the Eyes of the Forest." Oscar exhaled softly. "So, the lynx too are fearful of the woods, like us."

"I guess." Elsinore said no more. But this irrational fear that the beavers had of the cedar woods had always struck her as odd. She had her own theories. However, she kept coming back to one notion, and that was the Eyes of the Forest were the only unconquerable territory for the Castors. They had not been able to drown that mountain on which the ancient cedars grew. It had defied them for hundreds of years. Was this perhaps why they avoided it?

From her perch, Elsinore had a perfect view of the pond. She kept scanning for any sign of Dunwattle and his best friend, Locksley. There was a subtle pattern to the water when beavers swam beneath it. The deeper they went, the dimmer the pattern was on the still surface of the pond. As dawn approached, she had seen nothing. Heard nothing, except the thick snores of four dozen or more beavers at rest, deep into their slumber. But now, as first pink faded into the long gray, she did detect a pattern on the pond surface. Her perch was high above the water, so it gave her a good view that was vastly superior. And to enhance that perspective, she spread her wings and took flight. There were three patterns, actually, of three beaver kits whose hind webfeet weren't quite as large as those of grown-up beavers. It must be Dunwattle and Locksley, but who might be the third kit? They were heading to the east bank that had a long tunnel through which beavers could enter and exit the pond unseen. "All right," she murmured to herself. "Let's see where they're going."

But minutes later Elsinore was confused. She was sure that the kits had entered one tunnel that exited on the east bank of the pond. She had been waiting patiently now for close to an hour in a slender fir tree near the pond exit. The sun was climbing higher and higher in the sky, and yet no kit had emerged. Three times now she had flown down from her perch in the treetop to peer into the exit, but there was no sign of them. Where could they have gone? It was as if they had been swallowed by the earth. She was completely bewildered.

CHAPTER 34

Eyes of
the Forest

"We're not going straight anymore in this tunnel are we, Yrynn?" Locksley asked.

"No, we just bent south."

"I never knew this tunnel curved at all."

"It didn't until I made it."

"What do you mean, you made it, Yrynn?"

"Well, me with the help of the earthquake. I think the quake started it. I like the cedar forest, the Eyes of the Forest, but you know the superstitions. I wanted to keep coming back. So I dug this passage where no one would see me. It won't be long now, though, until we can come out right in the middle of the woods."

Both Dunwattle and Locksley felt a squinch in their

skeats. How could Yrynn talk so casually about this place that many had said was haunted? But then again, they had been in the most haunted place of all, feasghair, where souls could be doomed to wander forever.

"We're here!" she announced suddenly. "Now listen to me. When we crawl out, we shall be in the hollow of a tree, a tree that's more than three thousand years old."

"How do you know how old the tree is?" Dunwattle asked.

Yrynn tipped her head. "I'm not sure, actually. It just came to me."

She looked down at the bag of bones that Dunwattle had set down. "And let's not speak ill of wolves in the presence of Stellamara's bones."

The two kits nodded. "Yes, yes, of course, Yrynn," Dunwattle said.

"First we have to scramble over these roots. They run deep and they are all tangled up. But just try and keep climbing."

Soon a trickle of light pierced the darkness of the tangled roots.

"Almost there!" Yrynn called back.

And then they were there. They crawled out of the hollow in the base of an immense and gnarled tree and into the dappled sunshine of noon.

Elsinore skimmed high and then low over the surrounding countryside. She had crossed countless creeks and streams and one river, but there was no sign of the kits. It was as if they had vanished into thin air. She did however catch a fleeting glimpse of that pesky spiderlike thing she had seen when flying over the lower Tweed. She ducked into a thick grove of trees for cover. *Hmmph,* she thought. *Bet the kits went underground as well!* But they certainly couldn't stay there forever. Nor could she stay in this tree forever.

As soon as the spider thing had vanished and was nowhere in sight or ear-slit range, she emerged and began skirting the western edge of the cedar forest. Surely they had not gone there. The Castors were not normally a superstitious lot but were deeply apprehensive about that woods they called the Eyes of the Forest. The eyes weren't really eyes at all but merely dark knotholes in the immense trees. Would the kits have gone there? Would they have penetrated this mysterious forest where a strange breed of wolves was said to live? It was typical of the Glendunny beavers that they had told tales that this forest had never existed until the Canuck beavers showed up. Blame a Canuck, that was always the way. Rumors had been spread that these beavers had brought the seeds of these trees in their pelts. Total nonsense, of course. Elsinore was far from a tree specialist, but she did know that these trees were very old and had started growing on this mountain long before the Canucks had arrived. A century for a cedar tree was but a minute. It took several centuries, perhaps a millennium, for a tree to grow to the size of these giant trees. *Willful ignorance*, she thought, and sniffed.

She began to carve a turn to fly over the huge trees. Even with her keen eyesight, it was hard penetrating the thick leafy foliage of this forest at this time of year. She did however pick up a chittering sound below . . . a chittering that was definitely beaverish, yet another sound as well, a high-pitched noise that wove through the woods. She knew that sound! Lynx. *They must not see me!*

She folded her wings tight against her body and dived into the crown of a cedar. Carefully, almost daintily, she picked her way down to a lower branch. She could only hope that the dense foliage would camouflage her brilliant white feathers.

"You see, Grinfyll."

Elsinore's gut seemed to contract as she heard that name. Grinfyll! She had watched him for years. He had turned from an innocent ball of fluff into a wiry, taut creature of sharp teeth and muscle. Fleet and precise, he was a skilled assassin. He was born to kill.

Until Wanda, the beavers and the lynx had always existed almost side by side in a delicate balance of some sort, a kind of mysterious harmony that was not quite peace but perhaps accord. They had never taken on a beaver before Wanda. Their kills were mostly far from the pond. They lurked due south where there was a scattering of small cottage farms with chickens and young lambs to kill in the spring. They had also gone into small villages, killing stray cats and the occasional dog. But they had lived now in the forests near the pond for several years in this somewhat strained ease, a peculiar détente with the beavers and other inhabitants. It was never a hostile relationship, though sometimes tense. The previous Castor Aquariuses had always dealt with them skillfully. Fishing rights had even been extended to the lynx. They could swim but were rather awkward compared to beavers or otters. So what Elsinore was hearing now shocked her.

"We do not have the vote yet. But I don't think it matters. The Grand Aquarius is bound to come around. And if he doesn't . . . Well, it will just accelerate step two of our plan."

Elsinore did not need to hear the words. Step two would be killing Oscar. These were the kind of "miracles" that the brilliant engineer wrought. It was Snert's voice that drifted up to her in the cedar tree. First Dunwattle and then . . . Oscar. Great Cygnus! Snert of the Snout would become the Castor Aquarius!

"One by one, we'll get rid of them. And the Avalinda

line will end!" This voice belonged to Tonk.

What are they doing? Elsinore wondered. Taking over the pond, of course! That Dunwattle had been seen, the vysculf episode, must have only accelerated what they had long planned to do. They sought . . . Words failed Elsinore, and then she heard Snert's voice. He said the word. . . .

"Dominion!"

"Dominion!" Carrick now repeated it. "And we'll get rid of the Canucks."

"And what will I get out of this?" Grinfyll asked.

"What will you get out of it?" Snert said with mock wonder. "You, Grinfyll, my fine fellow, will get respect." He paused. "Not only respect but a title."

"What title?"

"Uh . . ." Snert thought a moment. "Commander in Chief of the Allied Forces."

"What does 'allied' mean?"

"Allied means to be joined, joined with us—the true beavers of Glendunny."

Then Tonk's voice could be heard. "Our heritage has been corrupted. Our blood is no longer pure. We will be purebloods, carrying the inheritance of those Castors from long ago Great Fosters."

Elsinore's head swirled. *True beavers?* What did that mean? Not evidently a Canuck. *Purebloods.* The very word made her feathers twitch and her gizzard wither.

"You see," Snert continued, "the fact that Dunwattle was seen is an unexpected blessing. It gave us our excuse. We shall have trials. Anyone who is a sympathizer of Dunwattle, anyone who voted against the curse of lynx shall become suspect. Suspect of disloyalty."

"And those dreadful Canucks will be the first to go," Carrick piped up.

"And," Tonk added, "I have been doing some research. I believe there might be a bit of Canuck blood in the Avalinda line. Precisely the Dunwattle branch, and possibly a maranth. You know there was a maranth that lived down near Great Fosters."

Elsinore almost staggered on the limb she was perched. Panic seized her. She did not know what to do. Could she swoop down on them? Break this up? But she was only one, and Grinfyll had eight lynx with him. In addition to the curse of lynx, there seemed to be two or maybe three lynx guards. And though her wings were strong, she only had two to battle with. There were at least four beavers there, and with their powerful jaws they could easily shred Elsinore if they tried.

She had to leave right away. She had to get back and warn Oscar, Elwyn, and whoever else in the Castorium would listen. But how many more of them were in on this plot? Just as she was about to lift from the branch into flight, a terrible screech splintered the air. She wheeled about and saw a lynx streak toward her from a lower branch—but not low enough. A searing pain tore at her shoulder. *My wing... my wing...* She felt herself plummeting. A swirl of blood and feathers spun through the air.

CHAPTER 35

A Spirit
Unbound

The three kits had arrived on a plateau in the cedar woods with the satchel of Wanda's bones and those of Stellamara, the unsettled spirits. The summit, a granite expanse at the very top of the cedar forest, was quite high. The kits felt as if they could almost touch the sky.

"So, now what do we do?" Locksley asked, looking up at the clouds that skimmed above.

"I think we just wait a bit," Yrynn said. "Not long. Perhaps we should lay out the bones here. I feel we are close to something, something between the sky and Great Pond where these spirits need to rest. Help me, Dunwattle, for they are your grammy's bones. It seems right that you should place those, and I shall place Little Blue's."

And so they did. Carefully, one by one, they pulled the bones from the bag.

"These are Little Blue's, I mean Stellamara's." Yrynn loved saying that name as she placed a tiny paw bone on the ground.

"And this long paw bone I think must be Grammy's," Dunwattle said. "Her fingers were so good for wattling, you know. I can remember them so well as she wove the wattling screens and then poked them in the mud—just so." He sighed. It was a strange puzzle that the kits were arranging but a meaningful one. A spirit puzzle, perhaps, and each shape, each piece was important. The two kits worked with reverence as they handled the cherished bones. Every gesture was a perfect expression of love, deep love and compassion.

"Maybe we should say a prayer," Dunwattle said. "Remember how Kukla said two-legs often made up these songs or poems that gave thanks to their god, like our Great Castor above, and spoke of love and how special something was?"

"What a lovely idea, Dunwattle. I think you should do it. I've always felt that you'll grow up to be a poet," Yrynn said.

"Really, Yrynn?" He opened his eyes wide. He had

written so many poems to her and yet never shown her one.

He clamped his eyes shut and tipped his head up.

"Dear Castor in the Great Pond or Neamorra or the Belong or the Creath Malach, we loved these creatures. Stellamara and my grammy Wanda. We shall always miss them, but take them to their heavens and help them feel the Belong—"

Just as Dunwattle was concluding the prayer, shrieks like shards of glass rained down as not one but two curses of lynx erupted from the brush and pounced on the three kits. The lost bones of the dead flew in the air. There was a terrible wailing. . . . *No! No! No!* It was the sound of ghosts crying. They were Wanda the Wattler and the ghastly yips of Stellamara. Dunwattle felt fangs sinking into his neck, and then there was a loud crack. Something roared in his ears. A sound that seared the air like a hot blade.

At the same time all three beaver kits found themselves suddenly snagged in a net of green light. They could not move. They felt paralyzed as a curse of lynx approached them with fangs bared. The horrible green glare of the lynx eyes snagged the three like the web of a venomous spider trapping an insect. The deadly light began to pour through them like that of a spider's poison. It was the luma! The luma of a lynx weakened the strongest, confused their brains, and destroyed their will. Each kit knew that they had to escape this scalding glare. They must charge, yet they felt themselves growing weaker and weaker.

Ah, the cool grace of darkness, Dunwattle thought as he longed for escape. *Is this what it felt like for Grammy? Am I dying now?*

The last thing that each would remember was this cool darkness.

Am I walking into the mouth of death? Locksley wondered.

Am I to embrace this darkness to find true light? Am I to surrender all? Yrynn wondered.

A tornado of violence swirled about them with gusts of blood and shrieks that ripped through the green iridescent veil.

Then finally there was silence, a thick silence. Exhausted and bloody, the three kits lay on the ground. Slowly they each opened their eyes. The luma was gone. They were breathing and bleeding.

The blue shadow of a creature approached. "Lie still, kits. You are wounded but will live. You resisted the luma. It drove them mad," a resonant voice spoke. It was like none other that Dunwattle had ever heard. "The sap of the cedar trees will mend your wounds."

As he spoke the shadows of legs, several legs, walked toward the three kits. And another little dark smudge seemed to dart in between the shadow legs.

"Stella?" Dunwattle gasped.

"Yes." The silvery pup now turned to the shadow. "Pa, they brought me back. I am with you again." Then the pup turned to Yrynn. "Nyarr is my father and he will mend you."

"But what about you, Stella?" Yrynn blinked. Was this the end of the story of Little Blue, a happy ending? For in fact Stellamara was a Rar Wolf and had at last found her father.

And just then another shadow appeared and crouched to nuzzle the pup.

"Mum, I'm back!" Stellamara said. "And my spirit kit, Yrynn. Mend her please and mend her friends, for they are my friends now. They found my bones."

And so, the wolf bent over and with her tongue began to lick the wounds of Yrynn with the sap from the ancient cedar trees. Other Rar Wolves stepped up to Dunwattle and Locksley and began to lick their wounds as well. And as they began to mend, the kits looked about and saw the unmended. The bodies of the curse of lynx and those of three beavers that had betrayed them: Snert of the Snout, Castor Tonk, as well as Carrick.

"We did that?" Dunwattle asked.

The Rar Wolf Nyarr stepped up. "You broke the luma,

and when you did, it scattered and the lynx became frightened and confused. They turned on the beavers and even on each other. So in the end they killed themselves."

Dunwattle looked about. Locksley, now sitting on his haunches, appeared stunned, a trickle of blood across his brow. And next to him was Yrynn. There was a tear in her shoulder fur. And though her fur was stained, it wasn't bleeding.

"But where are we?" Locksley asked.

"You are here in the cedar woods or the Eyes of the Forest, as you call it." The shadow spoke. It was indeed the shape of a wolf, an immense wolf.

"What happened?" Dunwattle asked.

"The end of 'once upon a time,'" the voice of a Rar Wolf said. "The end of the story of Little Wolf and Little Kit who had wandered afar from their lodge in the sky. They are home now."

Then another shadow spread over Dunwattle and seemed to softly pat his brow. "Grammy?"

"Yes dear."

"Am I dead?" Dunwattle asked.

"Oh no. I am dead but not you. Now I'm just on my way to the Great Pond, or Creath Malach, as the Rar Wolves call it here."

"But these other shadows? What are they?"

The large wolf called Nyarr came toward him. "We are Rar Wolves. We only appear as shadows to living creatures. This is our world. We are not dead. We are not ghosts. We are just shadows. Spirits. Spirits of stories lost. We are what stories are made from."

Other Rar Wolves were beginning to melt out of the woods into the small clearing. Their shadows appeared to dance across the granite rock.

"Follow me," the Rar Wolf Nyarr said. They followed the shadows to the edge of a steep precipice. A stiff breeze began to blow, and a mountainous bank of clouds rolled into the canyon below.

"This is the canyon of the dead," the Rar Wolf said. "It is not heaven; it is not feasghair. It is Nothingness. This is their hell. Nothingness." And the shadows of the Rar Wolves began to pick up the dead and drag them as they would drag prey and then they dropped them into the canyon. There were no sounds as the bodies dropped. It was as if they were falling forever into the Nothingness.

"B-b-b . . . but I don't understand," Dunwattle said, turning to Yrynn. He was unsure why he had turned to Yrynn. But it was Yrynn he had first seen go into the cedar forest.

There was a soft chuckle from Nyarr.

"We don't quite understand ourselves. This kit is different." He walked over to Yrynn and, raising a shadow paw, he put it gently on her shoulder. "This kit is bold. She walks where others do not dare. She believes where others stop thinking. And yet she thinks where others might not dare to believe. I think she has a bit of the shadow in her too."

West with the Stars

"**W**hen are we going to get there, Mum?"

"We'll get there when we get there."

The pup's sister, Edy, whispered, "That's what Mum always says, Iggy."

"Well, are we halfway there yet?" Iggy asked.

Their mother, Glory, turned to them and said, "We are all the way there!"

"Here . . . !" yelped Edy. "We're really here!"

They clambered out at the mouth of the river. The sun setting in the west cast a sparkling light over the greenest water they had ever seen.

"This, pups, is the Irish Sea!" Glory took a deep breath. "And now our real voyage begins. Come along. We must start right away. You see how the seagulls face us? That means they're facing into the wind, and that means the wind shall be with us." Her voice drifted off as she recalled a poem her own mother had often recited to her when they had traveled rivers together. She began to speak in a soft voice.

"The wind is at our backs
And ahead the sun's just setting
A land for us awaits
It's calling us back ... to Canada ... to Canada
Come back, you otters,
To the land where you belong
To Canada, to Canada, to the land for which you long
Can't you hear the water lapping
On the shores of Newfoundland
Can't you feel the breezes scraping
Against that rockbound coast
Or the blooming field of Bunchberry
Its white petals like the stars
And the stars in heaven shall guide us
Through darkest nights ahead
The gulls we shall follow
When the dawn breaks with light
We might catch a log and ride it
Or silently board a ship

But we'll get there, my dearest ones,
With courage, strength, and wit
Through storms we shall swim
We'll find fish to eat
We're tired of this old country
We must turn and face the new
No more drizzles in our soul
No more shadows of the lynx
To Canada we'll go
Then once on those shores
We'll watch the sun rise
On the far side of this sea
But from England we'll be free
Follow me, follow me. . . .

"Come, pups," she said softly. The little otter family waded into the salty waters of the Bight of Clyde and into the wide, wide sea of the Across.

AFTERWORD

Almost a decade ago I read an article in a British newspaper that the first beaver in more than five hundred years had been spotted in England. Not since shortly after the time Henry VIII went hunting for them from his Surry hunting lodge, Great Fosters, had any beavers been seen in the United Kingdom. The tabloids began screaming the news of the return of this vanished species. So that is how this book, *The Secret of Glendunny*, began. I was fascinated and I started, as I often do with my animal fantasy books, to read all I could about beavers—their natural habitats, their social behavior, their natural history, their biology. My fantasies always begin with facts.

What was most surprising to me was how vitally important beavers are to the environment. I had always thought them to be a destructive force in nature. What I discovered was quite the opposite. Beavers are crucial to the conservation of our continent, our very land. They are responsible, as one environmentalist explained, for our watercourses and the wetlands we will long for in the times of climate change. They have shaped our country. For those reasons beavers have been declared a keystone species. But many people consider beavers to be nuisances to the development of land for agriculture and housing. Furthermore, hundreds of years ago beavers were hunted for the value of their fur, resulting in their near extinction in Canada.

One of the most intriguing things I learned about beavers is the symbiotic relationship between those industrious creatures and swans. Swans often build their nests close to beaver ponds, as the kinds of weeds and aquatic plants that grow in those ponds are a favorite of swans. The tops of old beaver lodges provide perfect nests for swans. The swan in exchange can often signal danger for the beavers. If the beavers hear a sudden squawk or a screech from a swan or other birds that can signal danger, they will immediately dive deep into their ponds.

The reason I so love writing animal fantasy is that I can become a world builder. A world where animals do extraordinary things. A world where they quest for knowledge beyond their natural attributes. A world where they might experience a deeper emotional life than we humans could ever imagine. But the fantasy elements need to be launched from a basis of biological facts. We all know that despite their masterful engineering abilities that allow them to build dams and construct intricate lodges beavers cannot read or write. However, if I can create a creature who is totally believable, I hope I can bring readers to that famous brink of suspended disbelief. Yes! My beavers can do the unimaginable but only after I can understand them as a biologically unique species that has literally shaped America.

Some historical aspects of this story are true. There was a pond near the hunting lodge of King Henry VIII that was the habitat of beavers and the king hunted them. He loved their fur and one of his favorite dishes was beaver tail. Furthermore, swan meat was considered a wonderful dish by sixteenth-century people. So the king often helped himself to the swans that settled near the pond. The bird was usually roasted and then the wings would be reattached to the roasted body in a rather elaborate presentation.

It is also true that King Edward I of England, who also was known as Edward Longshanks and ruled from 1272 until 1307, was a brutal monarch. His first attempt to invade and conquer Scotland was in 1296. At that time King Edward stole the Stone of Destiny that was considered sacred by the Scots, as it had been used for hundreds of years for the coronation of Scottish kings. It was then built into a new throne at Westminster Abbey in London, and every monarch of England has sat upon it to be crowned. On Christmas Day of 1950, four Scottish students removed the stone from Westminster Abbey. Three months later it was found.

It is also true that Queen Elizabeth II technically owns all the unclaimed swans in open water in England and Wales. But the Queen actually exercises ownership on only certain stretches and tributaries of the River Thames around Windsor. The upping of the swans is an annual event where the swans of the River Thames are rounded up and rings placed on their ankles. Its purpose is to take a census of the swan population.

Bibliography of helpful books about beavers and swans:

Goldfarb, Ben. *Eager: The Surprising Secret Life of Beavers and Why They Matter.* White River Junction, VT: Chelsea Green Publishing, 2018.

Johnsgard, Paul. *Swans: Their Biology and Natural History.* Lincoln, NE: Zea Books, 2016.

Patent, Dorothy Hinshaw. *At Home with the Beaver: The Story of a Keystone Species.* Photographed by Michael Runtz. Berkeley, CA: Web of Life Children's Books, 2019.

Raum, Elizabeth. *Beavers Build Lodges.* Illustrated by Romina Martí. Mankato, MN: Amicus, 2018.

Runtz, Michael. *Dam Builders: The Natural History of Beavers and their Ponds.* Markham, ON: Fitzhenry & Whiteside, 2015.

Schuyl, Malcolm. *The Swan: A Natural History.* Ludlow, UK: Merlin Unwin Books, 2012.